The Reason Is You

Nikita Singh is the bestselling author of eleven novels, including *Letters to My Ex*, *Every Time It Rains* and *Like a Love Song*. She is also the editor of the collections of short stories *25 Strokes of Kindness* and *The Turning Point*.

After working in the book publishing industry in New Delhi for a few years, she got her MFA in Creative Writing (Fiction) at The New School in New York. Invested in the fight against climate change, she handles marketing for a solar energy company based in Brooklyn.

Nikita is a digital nomad, currently obsessed with travel, tea and thrillers. You can follow her adventures on Instagram and Twitter (@singh_nikita).

NIKITA SINGH

The Reason Is You

HarperCollins *Publishers* India

First published in India by
HarperCollins *Publishers* in 2019
A-75, Sector 57, Noida, Uttar Pradesh 201301, India
www.harpercollins.co.in

2 4 6 8 10 9 7 5 3 1

P-ISBN: 978-93-5302-669-1
E-ISBN: 978-93-5302-670-7

Typeset in 11.5/15 Minion Pro at
Manipal Digital Systems, Manipal

Printed and bound at
Thomson Press (India) Ltd

For
Tutu and Popo
— my little cousins, the bravest boys.

We're born with millions of little lights shining in the dark
And they show us the way
One lights up
Every time you feel love in your heart
One dies when it moves away

'All the Little Lights'
—*Passenger*

Chapter 1

As Siddhant shrugged out of the white lab coat and hung it up on the lone hook on the wall inside his locker, he felt the last of his energy leave his body. He tilted his head to the right, cracking a bone at the back of his neck – a bad habit he had picked up years ago, from sitting in front of a computer for several hours at a stretch while studying for his medical exams. He'd just finished a twelve-hour shift at the hospital, and what he wanted most was to shut his eyes and keep them like that for the next twelve hours.

However, he wasn't at liberty to choose to spend his evening sleeping. He had plans, ones that he had made when in a much more adventurous mood. But as always, when it was time to follow through, he regretted making them. He gathered his belongings and headed home.

For the past decade, every waking second of his life had been dedicated to building a life as a doctor. It had started in tenth grade, when his parents sat him down and had *the talk* with him; the talk about what he wanted from his life and what he was doing to achieve it. However, all parties involved understood full well that it was less about what

1

he wanted for himself and more about what they wanted from him, expected of him.

Siddhant's parents were doctors, and so was his elder brother. His life had already been chosen for him; he didn't have the right to opinion or decision-making. But he couldn't fully blame his family, could he, since he had never tried to express his opinion on the matter? True, he hadn't brought it up because he knew it would be futile, but he couldn't say that he'd tried to show his parents his perspective either. He'd simply accepted his fate and slaved away for a decade to get where he was today: a senior resident at AIIMS.

If he was completely honest with himself, he actually loved his job. As a perennially curious person, when he'd first started preparing for medical entrance exams, he'd found that the more he learned, the more he wanted to. His thirst for knowledge made him an excellent student; so even though the long hours and hard work were overwhelming, he couldn't deny the wave of satisfaction he felt at the end of every day. Practising medicine brought him fulfilment, so he tried not to complain too much. And anyway, his life was much easier now that he was a senior resident. Earlier, he had worked as a junior resident for two years, with eighteen- to twenty-hour shifts alongside tons of study material to wade through. In comparison, his life felt like a vacation now.

If only he had had the night to relax … But he didn't, so he needed to get over it. After all, he was going to have dinner with a beautiful girl, and word on the street was that being social and going out was a much better way to spend evenings than lying uselessly on the couch.

When he got home, he walked straight to his bedroom, avoiding looking in the direction of the couch and imagining himself having a cold beer in front of the television. He picked out a shirt and ran the shower. Within ten minutes, he was ready to leave.

Just as he was about to step out of the door, a voice called from behind him, 'Where are you going?'

'Date night,' Siddhant said. He turned around and saw his flatmate, Priyesh, come out of his bedroom, his dishevelled appearance indicating that he'd just woken from a nap. Siddhant couldn't help looking longingly at the couch.

'Right. This the doctor girl?'

'Yep.'

'Should I wait up?' Priyesh grinned, and then ducked behind the fridge door, fishing for something.

'Bye,' Siddhant drawled as he left, ignoring Priyesh's remark. Priyesh had the tendency to hide behind jokes when it came to uncomfortable topics, but while he was acting casually about Siddhant going on a date, they both knew that this was not a frequent occurrence at all. In fact, Siddhant hadn't dated at all since his break-up with Maahi, which was over a year ago. Maahi … Just thinking about her made his chest feel heavy … and he was suddenly grateful that Priyesh had made light of the situation instead of making a big deal about it.

When he arrived at the restaurant, Siddhant was happy to find that he was a few minutes early. The last thing he needed on a first date was to be late and have to make excuses. Besides, he liked this girl, and wanted to make a good first impression. Just as he pulled out his phone to check on her ETA, he saw her walk in through the door.

When Akriti caught his eye, she smiled a smile that reminded him why he'd asked her out to begin with. The kind of smile that was in equal parts genuine and childlike. Her eyes widened slightly as he walked towards her. When he reached her, she rose on tiptoe and hugged him lightly, her earrings jingling happily as she pulled away.

Siddhant had a strange out-of-body experience: he watched himself greet her by accepting the hug she offered, as if they were in a movie. When he pulled away, she was still smiling, which brought a smile to his face too, until he realized that he should probably say something. They couldn't just stand there indefinitely, grinning at each other like lunatics. He'd never done the formal dating thing, and his only frame of reference for what to do next was Hollywood movies. He racked his brain for something funny or interesting to say, and finally came up with a meagre 'Hi!'

'Hi, Sid. You look very handsome,' Akriti said, with another one of her smiles.

Right. A compliment – why hadn't he thought of that? She did look extremely pretty in her flowy dress with her wavy hair framing her face, but now he felt like the window of opportunity to compliment her had passed.

'Thank you,' he said. 'Should we go in?'

'Yes, let's,' Akriti said, taking his arm and purposefully walking inside.

They were definitely in a movie.

As they were shown to their table, Siddhant recalled what Prachi, their mutual friend from the hospital, had told him about Akriti – that she liked things *proper*. Everything planned out, done step by step and right. She'd warned him that it could be annoying to try and live up to the expectations rom-coms had set for Akriti, but so far, he found it cute.

Once they were seated, Akriti looked at him expectantly. He was required to say something, something interesting.

'You're making me nervous,' Siddhant said, resting his hands on the table and looking straight at her.

'I am?' Akriti looked confused. 'What am I doing wrong?'

'Nothing! I guess I just haven't done this dating thing in a long time, or ever, actually. Not sure how to …'

'Talk? Just use words.'

Her comment made Siddhant feel dumb. He didn't know how to respond to that, so he was quiet for a moment, before he asked, 'Um, how was your day?'

Akriti looked at him for a second, as though thinking, *really?* But then she said, 'It was all right. I assisted Dr Patel in a neurosurgery, so that was pretty cool.'

'That does sound cool. What was the surgery for?'

'It was a resective surgery for epilepsy. It was supposed to be pretty straightforward, but there were so many complications! One thing after the other kept going wrong. We were in there for like six, seven hours!' Akriti was now talking enthusiastically, which relaxed Siddhant.

'Was the surgery successful? Or are you waiting to find out?' he asked, his interest piquing.

'The charts looked fine when I left the hospital, but of course, we won't know till the patient regains consciousness.'

Siddhant nodded. 'Of course. Wow! I'm jealous. Dr Patel never brings me in on the interesting cases. Just the simple, boring ones. It's kind of ridiculous that he's one of the best we have in the country, possibly the continent, and all the time I've spent in surgery with him has been so incredibly dull.'

'But that's the thing, right? He does the high-profile cases with other high-profile doctors and lets us peasants assist only on the smaller cases. The only reason I got to scrub in on today's surgery was because it was *supposed* to be super straightforward.'

'Okay, answer me honestly,' Siddhant said seriously. 'You are secretly glad that the poor patient had multiple complications on the operation table, aren't you? Because you got to see Dr Patel's cool surgery moves?'

Akriti exhaled dramatically. 'No! That's *so bad*!'

'Absolutely horrible,' Siddhant said, shaking his head at her, his expression dead serious. 'Answer me.'

'No! No, I'm not …' Akriti protested, then said in a small voice, 'I mean, I did get to learn some cool procedures …'

'Dr Akriti Arora! You should be ashamed of yourself.' Siddhant admonished her grimly.

'But … but I didn't *cause* the complications! I'm just grateful for the opportunity it provided … I can help more people now that I've learned these techniques …' Akriti babbled, trying to defend herself, but gave up, looking genuinely concerned by his stern reaction.

Siddhant couldn't keep a straight face any longer. He burst out laughing. Akriti looked at him, taken aback. 'Don't look so miserable!' he said. 'All residents wish terrible things on their patients once in a while. It's the thirst for learning; I get that!'

'You're *awful*! Ugh you made me feel so *terrible*,' Akriti exclaimed, even though she looked quite relieved.

From that point on, the evening became a lot more fun. They both relaxed and talked animatedly about surgeries and doctors and spent a large part of the evening trying to determine who had assisted in cooler surgeries. A lot of good food was left to grow cold and be taken away as they barely took note of it, too immersed in their conversation.

Somewhere during the night, Siddhant realized that he really liked her. It was very easy to talk to her, even though it was the first time they were having a proper conversation with each other. They'd chatted for a few minutes at a couple of parties before this, and he'd liked her from a distance. But now, after spending hours together on their first date, he thanked himself for asking her out.

Just as he pulled out his wallet, Akriti's phone rang. She turned it face up on the table and frowned at the screen. Siddhant resisted the urge to look at her phone.

'Is everything okay?' he asked instead, busying himself with the check.

'Hmm,' Akriti murmured absently, her eyes still fixed on the phone, lit up, lying on the table.

'Akriti?'

'What?' She looked up abruptly, startled by his voice, as though she'd forgotten he was there. 'Yes. Yes, everything's fine.' She pointedly ignored her phone and offered Siddhant too-cheerful a smile instead.

Siddhant stared at her for a second, unsure. She seemed absent; it was as though her body was sitting in front of him but her mind had travelled far away in the past couple of minutes. He wanted to ask, but decided it was best not to prod because it was hardly his place. She would tell him if she felt like sharing, so he let it go.

However, the next second her phone lit up again, and this time, she picked it up instantly and said, 'Yes.' Her voice sounded unusually loud, very unlike the voice of the girl who had been joking and laughing with him just minutes earlier.

'What? I can't hear you … Hold on.' Akriti covered the speaker with her other hand and stood up. She mouthed, 'I have to take this outside,' and left when Siddhant nodded.

The next ten minutes felt exceptionally long to Siddhant because in that time he paid the bill and then sat there, watching the door for Akriti. Two different waiters asked him if he needed anything else, and both times he said no, thank you, and explained that he was just waiting for his date to return. For a wild second, he worried if she'd just decided to ditch him and make a run for it, but then he saw her purse hanging from the back of her chair and his moment of panic passed.

Twenty more minutes later, the annoyed looks from the people waiting to grab his table finally got to him, so he took

Akriti's purse and stepped out of the restaurant. He let her know in a text message that he was waiting outside for her, but when he didn't get a response from her in the next few minutes, he decided to walk around to see if she was still on the phone.

He felt mildly frustrated at her behaviour. Who leaves someone at the dinner table for half an hour without explanation? But then he remembered the distressed look on her face when she'd glanced at her phone and decided to give her the benefit of the doubt. It must have been an important or unpleasant call.

He didn't have to look too long; just as he turned the corner, he saw Akriti leaning against the wall, hunched over, as if it was a struggle just to keep her body from collapsing. His heartbeat quickened as he rushed to her side. Her body was shaking uncontrollably; she was crying.

'Akriti! What's going on?' Siddhant said, alarmed, in a voice that didn't quite sound like his own. He had run to her, but when he reached her, he didn't know what to do with his hands.

She shook her head, so he knew that she had heard him even though she didn't look up at him, or acknowledge his presence in any other way. Her head was still bent into her chest, her entire body curled into itself as she wept.

'What's wrong? Will you please tell me what's wrong?' Siddhant pleaded. He wanted to pull her up, but restrained himself. Even though he desperately wanted to help her, he didn't know her well enough or long enough to provide any physical form of comfort. Passers-by were now stopping to stare, and he looked around anxiously, trying not to wonder about how they were reading the situation.

Akriti continued to cry. These weren't the kind of tears one normally saw, caused by mild pain or distress. Her cries were deeper, as though coming from a very dark place inside of her, raw and gut-wrenching. It made him feel hopeless, like nothing would be right again in the world.

'Akriti,' he said, his voice tortured. He put his hand on her shoulder and gently coaxed her to rise. 'Akriti, please! What's wrong? Please talk to me …'

Whether it was the sound of her name or his touch, he didn't know, but Akriti finally turned her face and looked at him. Her eyes were ringed red, blotches of colour staining her face, betraying her anguish, even as she wiped away her tears. 'Siddhant …' she said, and fresh tears escaped her eyes and flowed down her cheeks, unchecked.

Encouraged by her acknowledgement of him, Siddhant helped her stand up. He held her in front of him, clutching her shoulders, supporting her weight. She was looking at him, her eyes locked into his, while the rest of her face crumpled as fresh waves of grief rocked her.

'What's wrong?' Siddhant asked. He spoke quietly but sternly. In order to help her, he had to first find out what had happened.

'That was my … my stepmother,' Akriti finally said, gesturing to the phone in her hands. Before she could say more, she broke down again, staring at her phone, almost as though she was scared of it. Her knees buckled.

'What happened? Is she okay?' Siddhant tightened his hold to keep her upright. 'Hey, Akriti, look at me, please. Is your mom okay? Did something happen to her?' His voice broke without warning, because as he said those words, a chill crept up his spine. His own mother wasn't exactly the warmest or most loving mom who doted on her son, but just the thought of something happening to her knocked the breath out of his body. The feeling was so sudden and shocking that he staggered, caught off guard.

'No … no, she's fine …' Akriti was shaking her head furiously. 'She's fine. She called … she told me …' She fell silent, as if she had no strength left to say the words, as if the words were too hard, too horrible to say out loud. Siddhant kept holding her, bracing himself for terrible news, giving her the time she needed to form the ugly words. Akriti shut her eyes. When she opened them, Siddhant was looking at her quietly, with concern, waiting for her to speak. As if drawing strength from him, she spoke again, the words rushing out of her. 'She said my dad had a cardiac arrest … that he didn't make it. He's gone. My dad's dead.'

She fell forward on his chest, gasping for air, and he held her as tightly as he could, while her body trembled violently with shock and grief.

Chapter 2

Siddhant went through the motions of getting himself and his stuff together, preparing for a long overnight shift at the hospital. He shoved his freshly laundered scrubs into his backpack, followed by his water bottle. He looked around his room absently for his keys. His mind wasn't in the room with him; it was hundreds of kilometres away.

'Oh, hey. I didn't realize you were home,' he said to Priyesh as he grabbed his keys from the kitchen counter.

'Just got back from the hospital,' Priyesh said, falling back on the couch and propping his feet up on the centre table. 'Today sucked.'

'What happened?'

'Lost two patients.'

Siddhant looked at his friend who was lying back on the couch with his eyes closed, his chest rising and falling slowly with deep, deliberate breaths. Siddhant had had many of those days himself and knew better than to ask for details.

'That really sucks,' he said shortly.

'Yep,' Priyesh said, opening his eyes. 'How's the girl doing?'

Siddhant shook his head. It had been ten days since the night Akriti's father died, and she wasn't doing any better than she had been the night they first heard the news. Every time they'd spoken on the phone since then, which was every day, just for a few minutes, she'd sounded as bad as that night outside the restaurant.

'That bad, huh.' Priyesh said it more as a statement than a question.

There was nothing to be said. Just thinking about losing one of his parents made Siddhant's throat dry. He couldn't even begin to imagine how terrible it must be for Akriti, losing her father without warning. As far as she knew, he was perfectly fine that morning. She'd spoken to him on the phone, and picked up no signs of an illness, not even a cough or a groan.

Siddhant had very few details about what had happened, medically. But he understood that it wasn't his place to inquire, especially given Akriti's current state. He wished he could do something to make her feel better, but there was nothing to be done in these initial days of mourning. Temporarily salving the pain wouldn't heal the wound caused by her father's untimely demise. All he could do was be there for her when she called on his phone, whenever that was, and cried.

But even though he took all her calls, and frequently called her himself to check on her, he always felt worse after hanging up, owing to his inability to help her in any way. He'd never been very good with words or expressing himself. He was raised in a household full of practical people who were fierce followers of reason and action. In this case, there was no logic involved, no real action to take. He found himself completely useless.

Feeling worse than he had all week, Siddhant made his way to the door, completely unexcited about the fourteen-hour shift ahead of him. 'See you later,' he called to Priyesh, who mumbled something back.

❦

Siddhant woke up in a cold sweat, his temple throbbing. He blinked in the darkness. What had woken him up? Was that a sound? He strained his ears, but heard nothing. Sitting upright in his bed, he looked around. As his eyes adjusted to the darkness, he was able to make out the vague shapes of the furniture around his room.

His phone rang suddenly, giving him a start. In the still night it seemed to be inordinately loud, and reflexively, he picked it up and spoke into it. 'Hello?'

'Siddhant …' came Akriti's broken voice from the other side.

'Akriti? What's going on?' He was suddenly wide awake, her distressed voice causing a jolt in his stomach.

'I don't know. I just … don't know what to do.' She was crying.

Siddhant searched for words to comfort her. 'I know it hurts so much right now, but you won't always feel this way … It will be okay, Akriti,' he said. 'Trust me, it will be okay …'

'Will it?'

'Yes,' Siddhant said with more conviction than he felt. 'You'll feel better tomorrow.'

'How do you know?' Akriti said, almost as a challenge.

'Because … because it's a new day. They always say time is a powerful thing … so maybe tomorrow you'll feel less sad.'

Akriti didn't speak.

'I know it hurts,' Siddhant spoke into the silence. 'It's supposed to hurt. What you're going through … I can't even imagine. I won't pretend to know how you're feeling, and how you're managing to go on, every single day. But you are. You're being so brave … It's okay to break down. You're in mourning, you need time to absorb it all, and be okay again … This isn't something small that can be pushed under the carpet. I know that your entire life has changed … but you'll make it. Trust me. You'll feel better tomorrow.'

Siddhant waited for Akriti to say something, and when she didn't, he lay back on the bed, his phone to his ear. He heard her breathing become erratic, and slowly turn into sobs.

'Akriti,' he muttered.

She cried for what seemed like hours. Siddhant stayed on the phone with her, sometimes silent, sometimes whispering words of comfort. He couldn't tell if he was making her feel better or worse, or if anything he said was even making sense to her. She would be quiet for a moment, then break down again. It was hard for him to determine what was making her cry or what he might do to help her stop crying.

But he didn't give up.

A long while later, she finally said something. One word.

She sniffed, paused, and in a barely audible murmur said, 'Thanks.'

Siddhant smiled. She was feeling better! He'd helped!

He felt happiness in her small moment of positivity. Akriti talked for a little longer after that. She told him that their house was filled with relatives, and everyone was asleep. Except for her. She was in her room, dreading the *terahvi* ceremony that would take place the following day to mark the thirteenth and final day of mourning rituals for her father. A lot of people had arrived from out of town to attend the *terahvi*. The thought of seeing them, and listening to them talk about her father was overwhelming. She didn't explain further, and Siddhant didn't ask, once again trying to be respectful.

They didn't stay on the phone too long after that. Akriti sounded much better than she had at the beginning of the call, so Siddhant felt like they'd made some progress. He let out a deep breath and closed his eyes, but it wasn't until the early hours of the morning that he finally fell asleep, having spent most of his night tossing and turning, trying not to think about the horror of losing someone he loved.

He thought about his parents, whom he hadn't seen for a year. He thought about his brother and sent him a text. As he slipped into an uncomfortable sleep, Maahi's face floated into his dream, jerking him awake. What if something happened to her? What if he never saw her again? What if the last time he ever saw Maahi was the morning they had broken up? His insides knotted painfully. He felt like he had to throw up.

He paced back and forth in his room, shaking thoughts of her out of his mind. He never permitted himself to think of her. They had broken up. She wasn't allowed in his thoughts. Because if he thought of her, and everything they had had together and then lost … *No, stop, there's nothing but pain there.* But what if something happened to her and he could never see her again … *STOP.*

So, he stopped. He had one year of practice; it wasn't as hard to put up his walls anymore.

❦

The following morning, Siddhant had a fully baked plan in his head – he was going to call in sick at the hospital. They were not going to be happy about it, and he'd definitely have to face his bosses' wrath when he returned to work the following day (but he couldn't worry about that yet – he would have to cross that bridge when he got there). Then he would board the first available flight to Amritsar and visit Akriti.

After their phone conversation the previous night, he knew that she needed someone beside her and even though he really couldn't take any time off from work, he had to prioritize this visit. This was important and couldn't wait – he had to be there for Akriti's father's *terahvi*. Despite what his parents had raised him to believe, his career wasn't everything.

He threw a change of clothes in an overnight bag and forty minutes later, was at the airport. Fortunately, he had a short wait until the next available flight, and to his pleasant surprise, he landed in Amritsar sooner than he'd imagined. As he walked out of the airport, he realized that he had no idea what Akriti's address was.

He called her, but she didn't pick up. In a moment of inspiration, he called their mutual friend, Prachi, who'd set them up. She did know Akriti's address but was surprised to find that Siddhant had gone to Amritsar to see her. That gave Siddhant a pause. For the first time that morning, he wondered if what he was doing was a little creepy. His intentions were good, but Akriti hadn't exactly asked him to come ... Was he intruding?

But he was already there, and he wanted to make sure that she was doing okay, so he pushed these thoughts from his mind and hailed a cab. He could tell it was the right place, even from a distance. There were rows of cars parked on the sidewalk, and as they drove closer, they saw hundreds of people collected under an open tent, outside a large four-storeyed mansion.

Apart from being wealthy, as was evident form the size of the mansion, the Aroras were clearly popular, judging by the number of people who had shown up to pay their respects. Siddhant got out of the car and looked around, unable to spot Akriti in the immense crowd. A few people glanced at him curiously as he slung his backpack over his shoulder and made his way towards the gate of the mansion.

He paused and looked around again, but before he'd finished scanning the crowd, he heard her voice. It was coming from somewhere to his right, and he followed it.

He saw her kneeling in front of an old lady, who was sitting in a chair with her face in her hands, and talking to her, trying to comfort her.

Siddhant hung back and watched her. She looked so small and weak, even as she attempted to help someone else with her pain. He waited till Akriti stood up and turned away, wiping the tears from her eyes. As she began to walk away, Siddhant stepped forward and called her name.

Akriti turned around at once. 'Siddhant!' she exclaimed. Her face changed into what started as a smile, but ended in a sob.

'Hey,' he said when he reached her. He found himself at a loss, wondering what to say. They'd only known each other a couple of weeks, and even though they'd talked on the phone every day since their date, this was only the second time he was with her. The last time they'd been together, she had cried on his shoulder. Now, surrounded by hundreds of strangers – her relatives, neighbours and acquaintances – he felt extremely conscious of how much of an outsider he was there.

But in the next moment, Akriti had thrown her arms around him, burying her face in his neck, and the awkwardness passed. 'You're here,' she said between sobs. She looked up at him and repeated, '*You're here.*'

'I had to come,' he said as if to defend himself. Then added softly, 'I couldn't let you … face this alone.'

Akriti held him tighter, with an urgency he had never known before, and Siddhant felt his ears burn with emotion. She was clinging to him in a way that showed him how happy she was to see him, and while that felt good, he was slightly embarrassed by how happy that made him feel.

He was very aware of the people around them watching them. Regardless, he snaked his arms around her and hugged her back. When Akriti finally pulled back, she looked up at him and smiled. Siddhant's heart melted. It was great to see her doing better … or at least comparatively better, given the grave circumstances. The way she had seemed every time they'd spoken on the phone had left him really concerned about her. He allowed himself to finally relax.

'What are you doing here? How do you even know my address!' Akriti said cheerfully. There were dark circles under her eyes, but her smile shone through.

'I woke up this morning, and I knew I had to be here with you today,' he said truthfully, ignoring how cheesy it sounded.

'That is just the most thoughtful thing …'

Siddhant shrugged, not good at taking compliments.

'No, it is! I never could've asked you to ditch the hospital for me, but I didn't even have to ask …' As Akriti said this, her expression turned more thoughtful. She studied his face, as if searching for some sort of sign. 'Thank you,' she said at last.

'No, don't thank me,' Siddhant said. 'It's nothing. I just … How are you doing? I was worried about you, because last night …'

Akriti nodded. 'Yes, yes, I know. I'm sorry if I scared you. I was … I felt like shit and didn't know who to call.'

'You can always call me.'

Akriti smiled again, and slipped her hand into his. 'Come with me,' she said, pulling him inside the house. She steered him through the living room and up two flights of stairs to reach what he knew immediately to be her room.

It was a large room painted in a dull shade of pink, with a round white bed in the dead centre, encased within delicate net hangings. Every inch of the wall on his left was covered with photographs. Everywhere he looked, he saw Akriti's face – at different ages and places, with friends, with a man who was clearly her father, selfies, smiling, sticking her tongue out. He turned to the girl beside him and grinned.

'Don't judge!' Akriti said. 'I was a cheesy teenager. So, what?'

'I didn't say anything!'

'You didn't have to! I can see you standing there, silently judging me. And this is not even the worst of it! You haven't seen my posters yet.'

Siddhant followed her gaze to the wall on his left. This wall was also hidden, but behind dozens of posters of the Spice Girls, Britney Spears, NSYNC and some other musicians and bands he didn't recognize. A little 'wow' escaped his mouth.

Akriti punched his arm playfully and pulled him to a couch that was propped against the closed window. They sat down, and exhaled together. They were quiet for a few minutes after that. A kind of awkwardness settled between them. They were suddenly alone in a corner of her room, probably the only people inside the house while hundreds gathered outside. In the distance, they could hear women wailing. A particularly loud cry pierced through the walls, and made the hair at the back of Siddhant's neck rise. He couldn't bear the silence between them anymore.

'Is your mom okay?' he asked.

Akriti nodded.

Siddhant nodded back at her, and they fell silent again.

'This is weird. Like … a sanctuary,' Akriti said.

'What do you mean?'

'*This*. Us. Sitting here alone, quietly. While outside … it's the exact opposite. Complete chaos.'

Siddhant looked at her. 'Are *you* okay?'

'I'm better now,' Akriti said sincerely, looking him in the eye. 'This moment feels so surreal to me, like … like you're saving me or something.' She laughed out loud. 'Sounds so cheesy, but you know what I mean? It feels like a refuge, away from all that madness and sadness.'

'I know what you mean.' Siddhant thought about how his heart had raced when he first saw the crowd. It had all felt *real*, all of it, all together. There were so many people, so many tears.

'Here, sitting alone in this corner with you, this feels so much … safer. Thank you for coming.' Akriti stretched her arm and clasped his hand in hers. She looked straight ahead, away from him.

Siddhant noticed her lower lip tremble, and held her hand tighter in his.

Chapter 3

Over the next few weeks, Akriti slowly seemed to return to normal. Siddhant felt less and less nervous around her, not as worried about her mental health anymore. She would still call him in the dead of night, sometimes on the brink of tears, sometimes already hysterical, but it was he who had encouraged her to do so. He had offered his constant support, telling her to call him whenever she felt the need to. She had resisted at first, but he insisted – for her sake and for his own peace of mind. He much preferred to be around and help her than imagine her dealing with this on her own.

But it was not easy on Siddhant. Apart from the emotional toll the relationship took, he ended up becoming dangerously sleep-deprived as well. Which is why when Siddhant had the rare day off on his schedule, he knew what he wanted to do most: take a long, long nap. He slept through the day, knocked out for several hours and woke up feeling completely disoriented. It took him several moments to realize that it was a little after six in the evening, that he was alone at home and that his stomach was growling with hunger.

Addressing the most compelling emergency first, he ordered dinner online and jumped into the shower. Ten minutes later, he emerged from the bathroom in a towel, and noticed the screen of his phone light up. His heart beating a little faster, he checked to see if it was Akriti. It turned out to be just a news update, and his whole body unclenched.

He couldn't help feeling a little selfish. After many weeks of balancing long shifts at the hospital and being available for Akriti, he felt protective of his one day off. He wanted to be carefree, just for a few hours. Stream crappy TV shows, play video games and be generally unproductive for a night – he'd forgotten what that felt like.

He fell backwards on the couch and turned the TV on. He had barely started browsing when the doorbell rang. He leaped up excitedly and swung the door open, only to find Priyesh waiting on the doorstep.

'Forgot my key,' Priyesh said in greeting.

'Thought you were my food,' Siddhant muttered.

Like a robot, Priyesh walked straight to the couch and collapsed on to the cushions. He flexed his arm and groaned.

'Bad day at the hospital again?' Siddhant asked.

'I can't keep doing this, man. My carpal tunnel is worse than ever, and it's reached my neck. Every nerve in my body hurts. I haven't slept more than four hours a night in a month. Not cool.'

'You chose this life,' Siddhant said light-heartedly.

'I thought I'd be saving lives,' Priyesh retorted in a small voice.

'And you are. You're just having … I don't know, a bad streak?' Siddhant said sombrely. He knew that Priyesh was complaining only because his job hadn't been the most rewarding lately. Normally, the role they played in saving lives compensated for the physical toll and emotional turmoil that was part and parcel of being a surgical resident. But of late, Priyesh had experienced a string of losses. And every lost life struck harder than the last.

'Bad streak? It's been *weeks*! I can't do this much longer. I'm completely drained. And —' Priyesh began to say something, but then caught himself. 'Never mind.'

'What?' Siddhant pressed.

'I don't know, man,' Priyesh said, sounding defeated. Siddhant could tell that he was trying to appear laid-back to hide his true feelings. 'I don't think they should assign me patients anymore. Other doctors can actually help these people, save their lives. *Better* doctors.'

'Don't be ridiculous! You've either been getting impossible cases or facing unexpected complications – it's been one or the other every time. It happens to all of us sometimes. No one blames you for it, and you shouldn't either,' Siddhant said firmly.

Priyesh didn't say anything.

'Trust me. It'll get better in time. Don't think about it too much,' Siddhant added for good measure.

Priyesh nodded once and turned away from him, indicating the end of the conversation, but Siddhant noticed that he looked a little relieved.

The doorbell rang, and Siddhant's face lit up. 'Cheer up! Food is here,' he announced, reaching to get the door.

They set out the food on the centre table, and as the smell of spices wafted through the room, Siddhant saw a tiny smile appear on Priyesh's face. They put on a superhero movie and ate in silence. For several minutes, the only sounds they made were monosyllabic grunts in appreciation of the food. Once they were sated on butter chicken and garlic naan, the mood in the room lightened significantly.

'That was the best food I've had in a long time,' Priyesh said, as he unscrewed their second beers.

'I keep thinking I can't eat another bite, then I eat another bite. I have to physically remove all this from my vicinity,' Siddhant said. He got up and carried the leftovers to the fridge.

'Good idea. We can't be trusted around food.'

When Siddhant returned to the couch, they lay back with their beers and watched the rest of the movie. Siddhant checked his phone a few times and was relieved to find no new notifications. No one seemed to need him – it was blissful. He felt uncharacteristically relaxed, but also a little guilty. Once the movie ended, Priyesh declared his intention to go to his room and pass out.

'How's the girl, by the way?' he asked.

'She's okay now,' Siddhant replied. 'Been doing much better of late.'

'That's great. Okay, I really must pass out asap —'

Before Priyesh could finish, the doorbell rang for the third time that night.

They looked at each other for explanation, a sudden fear appearing in their eyes; neither of them was in any mood to be interrupted on their night of doing nothing. Priyesh went to open the door.

'Oh, hey, Akriti, right?' Siddhant heard him say.

'Yes, hi,' came the response.

His heart raced. Was she okay?

'Akriti?' he said, approaching her, as she entered the apartment.

'Hey,' she said quietly. She looked fine, the only visible sign of potential distress being her hair, which was frizzy in the front.

'Okay ...' Priyesh said, retreating. 'Good night, guys.' He smirked at Siddhant before disappearing into his bedroom, clearly triumphant that the unannounced guest wasn't there for him.

Siddhant turned his attention to Akriti. 'What's going on? Are you okay?'

'Yes, yes, don't worry. I'm fine,' Akriti said, smiling up at him. She placed a hand on his arm and continued, 'I just didn't want to be alone tonight.'

'Oh, right. Great!' Siddhant said, looking around in dismay. The apartment was in an advanced state of dishevelment. He was dressed in sweats and, mentally, was in no condition to entertain. On top of that, even though he and Akriti had talked a lot on the phone in the past month, they'd spent very little time together, and this was the first time she had come to his place. He was completely thrown. 'Umm ... have you eaten?' he asked finally. That was a start – they could go somewhere to eat; that would take the pressure off him. He'd just eaten a *lot* of food, but he could eat again …

Akriti laughed. 'I have! Don't worry – you don't have to entertain me or anything! We can just … chill here.'

'Right. Of course.' Siddhant grabbed the stray pieces of clothing adorning the back of the couch in an attempt to quickly tidy up the space.

'Or we could go to your room,' Akriti said.

Siddhant turned to face her, holding a pair of dirty shorts. 'What?'

'Your room. You know, your bedroom?' Akriti glanced at Priyesh's door and then met Siddhant's eyes again. 'So that we can have more privacy.'

Siddhant couldn't say that he'd seen this coming. Nor did he understand what her intention was behind inviting herself to his room. He tried to think back to the last time they'd spoken, which was in the morning … She'd sounded a little sad, but mostly okay. There had been nothing to indicate that they would be spending time alone in his bedroom later that night.

'Okay,' he said, leading the way.

'So, how was your day?' Akriti asked, following him inside. She seemed quite at ease, which Siddhant found odd for some reason. This was definitely out of character for her. Something wasn't quite right …

'Not bad. Didn't do a whole lot. Had the day off, so I took a long nap.'

'That sounds nice.'

'It was. Can't remember the last time I slept so peacefully—' Siddhant stopped speaking abruptly, noticing the look on Akriti's face and realizing how his statement could be misconstrued. 'I didn't mean … I just meant I haven't had a day off from work in some time. You know how crazy our schedules are.'

'Yep. We have the same job.'

'Exactly.' Siddhant laughed nervously, wondering if he'd imagined the coldness in her voice. To be sure, he said, 'Hey, I'm sorry – I really didn't mean anything by it …'

Akriti paused for a brief moment, but then smiled. 'It's okay – I'm not mad! Don't worry about it. If anything, I'm grateful for all the sleep you've given up for me. I should be thanking you …'

Siddhant relaxed. He sat down next to her at the foot of the bed. 'No, no. You don't have to thank me. I'm glad I can help.'

'You're so sweet.' Akriti turned towards him and looked at him with genuine emotion.

'That's me!' he said, trying to laugh it off.

'My sweet boyfriend. How did I ever get so lucky?' Akriti leaned towards Siddhant and placed a little kiss on his cheek.

Siddhant was lost, wondering where the sudden affection was coming from … But it couldn't be bad, could it? No, it was probably a good sign; maybe she was actually getting better, returning to normal. And although a little unexpected, her display of affection was sweet.

He smiled at her. 'Stop it. I'm the lucky one.'

'Liar,' Akriti retorted and then fell backwards on the bed. 'I had a good day.'

Feeling more relaxed, Siddhant lay down next to her and looked at the ceiling. 'You did?'

'Yes … I mean, no, not at first. At first, I felt terrible. After I hung up the phone with you, I went to work, and then there was this case … this little girl had VSD … it was her seventh surgery this year and it was horrible. Her parents were so desperate, begging us to take care of their little girl …' Akriti was shaking her head. 'I couldn't even look them in the eye. It's so hard to keep the emotions out of it, you know?'

'Yes.'

'Anyway, the surgery was successful. I was only assisting, and honestly, I tried to take the back seat as much as possible. I couldn't have handled it if something had gone wrong … But in the end, the procedure went fine. She's okay for now.'

'That's all that matters,' Siddhant said quietly. He reached out and took her hand. 'Priyesh and I were talking about something similar earlier today. This job is always hard, but I think what really matters in the end is that we do our best.'

'Yeah, but what if my best isn't enough?'

'We can do all we can do, but that's all we can do.'

'That's a nice way to put it.'

'I just thought of it,' Siddhant laughed.

'So smart.' Akriti smiled, looking at the ceiling. 'You know that I really … appreciate you, right?' she said after a while. 'I do.'

'Okay, good. I need you to know that I'm not taking any of this for granted. You've been helping me through this really tough time … I can't even imagine what I would do without you—'

'You'd be fine!' Siddhant said. 'Really. You're so brave, and you've been so, so strong. I'm glad to be here, but you're underestimating your own strength.'

'A lot of that strength comes from you! I don't think I would've been brave at all if I were all alone in this. Just … learn to take a compliment, okay?'

They turned towards each other, their faces only inches away.

'Okay, I'm taking the compliment. I'm not very good at it though …' Siddhant said awkwardly.

'Clearly.' Akriti laughed. But a moment later, without warning, she lay on her back again and spoke sombrely to the ceiling. 'My mom died when I was ten.'

An 'oh' escaped Siddhant's mouth. He tried to gauge her expression, then said carefully, 'I heard a few people talking about it at the … at your dad's *terahvi*.'

Akriti nodded. 'She was in a car accident … on her way to pick me up from school. I took the bus normally, but we were going to go see a movie after school that day, so mom was gonna pick me and my friends up. We waited outside the school for so long, for what felt like hours, but she never came.'

Siddhant held her hand tighter, his throat tight, imagining a little Akriti waiting excitedly outside her school for her mother …

'It was so sudden, so unexpected. It broke our whole family. She died immediately, and so did the baby she was carrying. It was all over … just like that. I remember that night, when my dad begged me to eat dinner, I kept wondering why he wasn't acting all strong and putting up a brave front for me. He was crying openly. Howling. That sound … I've never heard anything so … so bone-chilling in my entire life. Our whole world was shattered. We were going to be a big family – I had prayed for a younger brother or sister for so long, and it was finally going to happen. We were all so excited, but then, it was just gone. Poof.'

Siddhant was now sitting up on the bed, holding both of Akriti's hands in his. He couldn't look away from her face, which was oddly blank, minus the slight tremble of her lower lip, and eyes that threatened to water any second. Siddhant wanted to comfort her. 'I can't even …' His voice caught.

'My dad and I became best friends. He was all I had, and I was all he had. We were each other's whole world; everyone else was gone. We had this deep bond, a very special connection … we were each other's most important person. No matter who else came into our lives, that would never change. And even when someone did come into our lives, well, *his* life, our bond didn't change. He found a new woman … way too soon. They were married within three years of my mom's death. The worst part was that it was like … like he was trying to get me a new mom, to *replace* my mom. I know he had the best intentions at heart, and that he probably fell in love with this woman or whatever, but to be honest with you, I didn't care at all. I still don't. I never loved her, but for the sake of my father, I never hated her either. She's no one to me and I've never let her presence in his life bother me.'

Akriti looked away from the ceiling and directly at Siddhant, and he couldn't decide if he should speak, and if he did, what the right thing to say would be. Before he could speak, she turned to the ceiling again.

'I already have a mom. She's dead, but she's my mom. This woman isn't. My dad wanted a wife, so he got himself one, but I didn't want her. Anyway, it doesn't matter. I never let her come between us. My dad and I had the same special relationship our whole life. We came to a silent agreement that I would never accept her, and he would never push it. I am not mean to her or anything; I just pretend she's invisible. And now that dad's dead, she's dead to me as well. I don't even know why we're talking about her. It's him I miss. I can't tell you how much I miss him. It's a permanent stitch in my chest. Never goes away. He was the most important person in my life, the only person who mattered, who was always there for me … and now he's gone. I have no one.'

'That's not true,' Siddhant said automatically, his heart breaking for her. 'You're not alone.'

Akriti finally looked away from the ceiling and at Siddhant. A fat teardrop escaped the corner of her eye. 'You …' she said. 'I can't thank you enough.'

'Don't thank me at all! Are you kidding me? It's terrible that you've seen so much sadness in your life … experienced so much loss. You deserve people who care about you. And I care about you so much. I want to see you happy. Please don't disrespect me by thanking me!'

'I love you.' She said it suddenly, without hesitation. And then, in one swift, assured motion, she pulled him down towards her by the collar of his shirt while her head left the bed and met him halfway as she kissed him. Her lips were soft and warm against his, her eyes closed.

Siddhant's body went numb. He couldn't think. He tasted her lips, pressed against his, he felt her open palm against his cheek, he heard her troubled breaths. Slowly, behind the fog of numbness, a sliver of panic rose. *He couldn't say it back. He couldn't say 'I love you' back.*

As the shock faded and he began to regain his senses, he slowly pulled away from her, breaking the kiss. Looking at her, he saw something – confusion? expectation? sadness? – flicker in her eyes. Panicked, he quickly leaned towards her and planted a kiss on her forehead. He tried to speak, but failed to summon any words that would help either of them.

Instead, he kissed her forehead again, before falling back down next to her. She didn't say anything either, so they lay there, holding hands, staring at the ceiling. He was awake long after her breathing slowed down and she fell asleep. He turned to look at her, wishing he could do something to take away some of her sadness.

He would do a lot of things for her, but he wouldn't lie to her about loving her.

Chapter 4

Three weeks later, Siddhant woke up to his alarm ringing incessantly in his ear. He'd already put it on snooze four times, and couldn't afford a fifth. Reluctantly, he got out of bed, and like a robot, headed straight into the shower. It was only when he emerged from the bathroom that he saw a single white rose on his bedside table.

'Akriti?' He looked around for her, but she was nowhere in sight. He couldn't remember if she'd said she had an early shift, and made a mental note to thank her for the rose when he saw her at work.

In the weeks following Akriti's sudden declaration of love for Siddhant, it was never brought up again, even though the memory was vivid in Siddhant's mind. They saw each other practically every day. If they didn't see each other at work, they met up afterwards, and as far as Siddhant could tell, everything was okay between them.

Of course, he wasn't foolish enough to believe that she had forgotten what she had said to him that night, but he wondered if she had realized later that she wasn't really in love with him, at least not romantically, not yet. They had

35

shared an emotional moment, and in the heat of it, she'd said something she probably didn't mean seriously.

Whatever the case, she didn't bring up the topic and neither did he. She seemed to be doing rather well, and he was really enjoying her company. They had grown more comfortable around each other. They were going out very frequently, and on nights that they were too tired to hang out with the rest of the world, she would come over and they'd order take-out.

Siddhant was still constantly surprised by her courage. In the two months since her father's unexpected death, Akriti had come a long way. When Siddhant looked at her now, he could only see a small part of the broken girl he had seen in Amritsar. There were days when they didn't talk about her father or her family at all. He made sure she knew he was there for her anytime she needed him, but he was too happy to see her smiling to bring up sad memories.

'Wanna carpool?' Priyesh hollered from the living room.

'Give me a minute,' Siddhant called back. He did a final phone-wallet-keys check and emerged in the living room a second later. 'Let's go.'

Priyesh gave Siddhant a sideways glance as they walked to the car. 'What are you smiling about?' he asked.

'Nothing. Was I smiling?'

'Like an idiot.' Priyesh looked annoyed with Siddhant's apparent happiness.

'Sorry!' Siddhant laughed.

'What, are you in love or something?'

'Dude, I smiled. Big deal. Let it go.'

On the drive to the hospital, Siddhant figured out the reason behind his idiotic smile. He was genuinely happy. He wouldn't go as far as saying that he was in love, but maybe he was starting to fall ...

He didn't want to dwell on it.

He didn't get the time to do so either. Soon after they arrived at work, there was an emergency case they were both put on. The operation lasted the entire day and took everything Siddhant had to offer. When it was finally over, he gobbled some mediocre cafeteria food while texting Akriti to see where she was.

'Oh man, I'm gonna pass out,' Priyesh complained, shoving large spoonfuls of food into his mouth.

'Yeah, you look delirious. Like you're drugged or something.'

'I feel drugged too. We should just take a cab now and pick up the car tomorrow. Your girl coming?'

Siddhant picked up his phone. Akriti hadn't texted him back. 'She didn't say ... I think she went home already. Let's just go. I'll drive.'

Priyesh fell asleep on the way and woke up with a start when they arrived home. They made their way up to the apartment without a word and parted ways in the living room.

Siddhant checked his phone again, hoping to see a message from Akriti, but found that his phone was dead. He plugged it in, intending to call her before falling asleep, and fell face-first on his bed. A few minutes later, before his phone was sufficiently charged to be turned on, he had dozed off, still clutching it.

🌹

The following day in the hospital, he looked for Akriti again, and learned that she hadn't come in. Nor had she come in on the previous day. Panic rising in his chest, he pulled out his phone and called her.

'Pick up, pick up,' he muttered as it continued to ring at the other end.

He only had a few minutes before he had to scrub for surgery, but he desperately wanted to talk to Akriti and make sure she was okay before he was cut off from the outside world for hours on end.

'You coming?' Dr Mehta asked.

Siddhant looked up. 'Yes. Yes, I'm coming.' He put his phone away and joined Dr Mehta and two other doctors. They went over the procedure for the surgery, and Siddhant had to push away worrying thoughts about Akriti from his mind. Before they went in, however, he excused himself for a minute and sent her a text message.

Hey, heard you didn't come in today. All okay? Sorry couldn't call last night – phone died. Heading into surgery now, will call after. Please text me that you're okay.

As soon as he entered the operation room, all thoughts unrelated with surgery disappeared from his mind. He was assisting two of the best doctors in the hospital, which was a rare learning opportunity, and he tried to absorb as much information as he could.

Despite the nine straight hours they spent in surgery, when they finished and stepped out, Siddhant was exhilarated. Surgeries like this reminded him why he loved his job. Apart from the chance to learn new techniques from the best minds in the field, and the thrill of saving someone's life, there was an unexplained pull he felt towards this profession. It was challenging, it demanded everything he had, but the payback was far greater than the investment.

As he changed in the locker room, he picked up his phone and checked for messages, but there was nothing from Akriti. His fears came rushing back. He called her immediately, but her phone was turned off. Once he was dressed, he located her friends, but they hadn't heard from her either.

Wiping sweat off his forehead, he considered his options. Who else could he ask? Should he go over to her place? She was probably just fine. In the time that they'd known each other, they had barely gone thirty-six hours without talking to each other until today, but that wasn't necessarily a reason to panic. When he had last seen her, she had seemed okay. She had stayed over at his place that night, but disappeared the following morning, without a word, leaving a rose on his nightstand. He had assumed that she'd had an early shift, and maybe she did, but it was very unusual for her to not show up to work for two days without a word to anyone, let alone just him.

It was clear that something was wrong, and ten minutes later, he found himself driving to her place.

Akriti lived alone in an apartment in south Delhi, and when Siddhant reached her building, a feeling of dread rose like an ugly snake in his chest. He took the elevator to her floor, trying to calm himself. When he rang the bell, no one answered. He waited anxiously for a few minutes, bile rising in his throat. Just as he began contemplating asking one of the neighbours, the elevator doors opened behind him. He turned around to see Akriti step out, carrying three supermarket shopping bags.

She stalled when she saw him, and a soft 'Sid' escaped her mouth.

'Where have you been?! I was looking all over for you,' Siddhant said, rushing to her.

'Out shopping,' Akriti said shortly. She walked calmly to her door and set the bags on the floor.

'Shopping? Where?'

Digging into her handbag for keys, she asked, 'Where? Do you want the names and addresses of the stores I get my groceries from?'

Siddhant paused. He couldn't read her mood. He sensed that under her calm demeanour she was angry. 'No, of course not. I was worried, that's all.'

'Worried. Why?'

He followed her inside and watched her put her things away. 'Because I didn't know if you were okay. I haven't heard from you in two days!'

'I called you last night but your phone was switched off.'

'I'm sorry, that's my bad. My phone died and I put it on charge but I was so tired from work that I just passed out,' Siddhant explained hurriedly. 'I was going to call you, really.'

'Sure. Doesn't matter.'

'No, it matters; I should've called you last night. I'm sorry. I tried calling this morning before surgery, and then again after surgery. Your phone was off …'

Akriti didn't look at him. She simply shrugged and said, 'My phone died.'

Siddhant was at a loss. She was clearly angry with him, but he didn't know why, or even how to make it better. 'Are you okay?' he asked plainly.

'Yes.'

'Are you sure?'

'Yes.'

When Akriti was done putting away her groceries, she walked into the kitchen and poured herself a glass of water. It was as if he wasn't even there. He decided to give her some space, let her adjust to his sudden appearance in her home. He sat down on the living room couch from where he could see her in the kitchen, busy moving things randomly. It was several minutes before she came to him.

'What's your plan?' she asked, looking bored.

'My plan?'

'Yes. How long do you plan to stay here? Because I have to go to bed.'

Siddhant stood up. 'Are you kicking me out?'

'I'm just asking if you have a purpose behind being here.'

'I do. I want to talk to you, and I want to make sure you're okay,' Siddhant said. Before she could protest, he added, 'And don't say you're fine. Because I know you're not. You're mad at me. So, tell me, what did I do?'

'Nothing.' She said it quietly, and he detected a change in her tone. She was warming up to him.

'Akriti.' He held her arms and pulled her closer to him. 'Look at me.'

She looked up, her face still impassive.

'What's going on? Tell me,' he coaxed.

'Nothing.'

'Something,' he insisted. 'I've been freaking out – I couldn't find you, you weren't at work, your phone was off. We haven't spoken in two days. I was losing my mind.'

Akriti jerked her arms out of his grasp and said heatedly, 'Why do you care, *friend*?'

'What?' Siddhant was completely taken aback.

'I haven't talked to any of my other friends in two days either. They're not barging into my home demanding an explanation. Why can't you and I go two days without talking to each other, friend?' Akriti was positively breathing fire.

'Because we don't … We talk every day …' Siddhant said, trying to figure out where this was coming from. 'It's different. We're not just friends, we're more than that.'

'Oh, we're not? Did I make a mistake with the *white* rose then? I wasn't aware we were more than just friends. When did that happen?' Akriti challenged.

'From the beginning! The first time we hung out, it was a date. We weren't hanging out as friends. You know this.

What's going on?' Siddhant tried to take her hand, but she walked away from him.

'What's going on is that you don't give a fuck!' If she had intended for that to sound emotionless, she failed. Her voice was shaking.

'What are you talking about?! I care about you so *so* much. I've told you that so many times. I don't understand what's happening here.' This time, when he grasped her arm and turned her around to face him, she didn't resist. 'Akriti, what's going on?'

She looked up at him with sad eyes, tears streaming down her face. 'You don't love me.'

Siddhant froze.

It took him several moments to recover. Their eyes were locked. He put everything that had happened since she had said 'I love you' in chronological order and tried to make sense of it all. It was like trying to work through a puzzle. Had she been pretending all this while to not care about the fact that he hadn't said he loved her back? Was the white rose a passive aggressive gesture, a sign? Did she actually mean what she had said that night, and was upset with him for not feeling the same way about her?

She loved him. That was it – she loved him, and she was angry that he hadn't expressed the same feelings for her. She was watching him with such misery in her eyes. He hated to see her unhappy. He gulped.

'I love you,' he said quietly, his eyes still locked with hers.

'Really?' Akriti let out a laugh-cry.

'I'm sorry I didn't say it sooner.'

She jumped up on her toes and hugged him in excitement.

He held her, his heart in turmoil. He let her face fall into her hair and said, 'Promise me you won't think like this anymore. You're not unloved and I do care. Please don't lock me out like this again. It's a terrible place to be; I felt so … helpless and terrified. We're on the same team. Please let me in and share whatever's going on with me so I can try to help.'

Akriti hugged him tighter and whispered, 'I promise.'

Chapter 5

'You should've seen Dr Mehta in surgery today. I've never seen so many things go wrong simultaneously. It was a perfect storm,' Siddhant said. He took a hurried gulp of water and resumed, 'But man, he did not panic or even hesitate for one second. He was like a superhero in there, putting out one fire after the other without so much as a crease on his forehead.'

'Sounds fun,' Akriti said gloomily, playing with the food on her plate.

'It really was,' Siddhant continued, his excitement unfaltering. 'Ah, man, this is what I got into this profession for. Priyesh, you know what I mean, right?'

'Dude, I'm just happy my patients don't keep dying anymore,' Priyesh said, without looking up from his food.

They were sitting in the hospital cafeteria. Even though Siddhant's shift was over and he was free to go home, he had wanted to hang out with Akriti before heading out. Both Akriti and Priyesh were working overnight shifts, and neither of them was particularly pleased about it.

'Your patients keep dying?' Akriti looked curiously at Priyesh.

'Kept, past tense. For a whole month. It was horrible.' Priyesh shook his head, his eyes wide, as if he was remembering an especially bad case. 'Thank God it's stopped. I was this close to giving up medicine.'

'He thought he was killing them,' Siddhant interjected.

'Like, on purpose?' Akriti asked.

'No, more like a jinx or a curse of some sort that he couldn't shake off. And it's weird, because for a second there, he really did believe there was an inexplicable supernatural element to it. He would get a straightforward case, and unforeseen complications would arise out of thin air.'

'You have no idea!' Priyesh said. 'And I'm a man of science, I don't believe in hocus-pocus, but you can't deny that they stopped—' he lowered his voice before continuing – 'the patients stopped dying on my table once my mom had that puja done at home.'

'Oh, come on!' Siddhant groaned. 'Not this again!'

'You *cannot* be serious!' Akriti exclaimed. 'There's no way there was any connection between patients losing their lives and your mom's puja!'

Priyesh evaluated his position for a second, looking from Akriti to Siddhant, before saying, 'Let's put it like this: I don't think that the puja helped, but I don't think that it didn't either.'

'Dude—' Siddhant began, but Akriti put her hand on his arm.

'This argument could go on forever. Let's just drop it,' she said. 'Besides, we've gotta go. Ugh, I hate overnight shifts. And don't say *I chose this life*!'

'I wasn't going to!' Siddhant defended himself.

'He was,' Priyesh countered, laughing. 'It's his favourite thing to say.'

'You do say that a lot,' Akriti seconded Priyesh.

'Fine, I do. But it's only because it's so challenging … I have to keep reminding myself that I chose this life and while the lows are really low, the highs are incomparable,' Siddhant said. 'Exhibit A: the surgery with Dr Mehta today. I don't even mind how under-rested I am right now, because that surgery was out of this world.'

'There he goes again …' Priyesh said, getting up.

'Don't listen to him; he's just jealous because he has to do clinic duty tonight while you worked on a cool case with rock star doctors all day,' Akriti said, rising. She kissed the top of Siddhant's head and said, 'Gotta go. Love you.'

Siddhant met Priyesh's eyes for a split second, before he turned to Akriti and said, 'Love you too.'

'Good night!' Akriti said, before walking away with Priyesh, leaving Siddhant sitting alone at the cafeteria table.

It had been a month since he'd said 'I love you' to her, but every time it was said, it still gave him a tiny jolt. Akriti had formed a habit of saying love-you to him, while hanging up the phone, while texting him good night and, like that night, while parting ways at the hospital. On an average, she said it to him 3.5 times a day. In turn, Siddhant was left with no other choice but to say it back to her 3.5 times every day too.

He was mostly okay with it; he liked spending time with Akriti, and they were now very comfortable around each

other. But sometimes, he saw her, and he had this thought …
that he didn't know her at all.

When the casual love-you exchanges first started
happening, Priyesh had asked him what was up. Siddhant
had refused to entertain him and told him that it was no
big deal. Maybe Akriti was a little emotional, but it was
completely justified, given the loss of, essentially, her entire
family. Maybe in her current emotional state, she needed
him more than he needed her, but it hardly meant that he
wasn't in this relationship willingly. He had to excuse the
little things and give her a break – and see the best in her.

Siddhant shook these thoughts from his mind and took
his tray to the trash can. He had had an excellent day at work.
And even though it had been a very long day, he was far from
tired. He felt energized. Surgery really was his calling. And
he felt fortunate to have found his purpose.

As he made his way to the parking, he had a smile on his
face. He got into his car and as he drove away, he watched
the hospital in his rear-view mirror. An imposing structure,
lit by hundreds of lights at night, it looked like home.

A few days later, driving away from the same imposing
structure, Siddhant laughed at how much it didn't feel like
home anymore. He had a strange love–hate relationship
with his profession. And he quite conveniently blamed the
bad days on his family – his overachieving parents and elder
brother, all of whom were exceptional surgeons, and this
had left him with only one career path.

It was especially easy to blame them on this particular
day given the exhaustion he was feeling following his shift,
on top of which his parents were on the phone, asking him
questions about his career plans. The Bluetooth speakers
surrounding him made their presence eerily real in his car.

'Oh, don't you go following that man's footsteps. Lunatic –
that's what that Mehta is,' his mother said. 'There are plenty
of other doctors in that hospital better suited to provide
you mentorship. I'll talk to someone and set up a meeting.'

'Maa, I don't need you to do that!' Siddhant protested.
'Thank you, but I don't need mentorship—'

'Don't be ridiculous; you're a surgical resident. Of course
you need mentorship!' his mother said in a reprimanding
tone. 'Good mentorship can and will change your entire
career. Surely, you cannot be too arrogant to think that you
don't need help at this very early stage of your career?'

'Of course not! That's not what I meant. I just meant I
don't need your connections at the hospital to mentor me.
This place has been my entire life for almost a decade now
– I have my own connections.'

'Well, if that's the argument you're choosing, then that
hospital was our life for over three decades!' his mother
retorted. Then, in a lower voice, she said, 'Isn't that right?
Tell your son!'

'Your mother is right,' Siddhant's father spoke reluctantly.
He rarely participated in their arguments, happy to be an
innocent bystander until called upon as a witness.

'Yes, but you don't understand – I have actual relationships
with the doctors here. Real … for the lack of a better word,
chemistry. Do you really expect me to randomly pick

someone to mentor me based on their relationship with my parents?' Siddhant asked.

'Chemistry? *Chemistry?* We're talking about your career here. Oh, goodness, I don't know what I'm going to do with you.' His mother's tone was, as usual, exasperated and defeated.

Siddhant didn't say a word. There was no reasoning with her. She was an extremely stubborn woman, used to getting her way – which helped her tremendously in her career, but as a mother, not so much. When she was in one of her moods, and wanted something to happen a certain way, arguing with her was pointless. She would nitpick and deliberate on the smallest, most insignificant detail, which would make the other person look like an idiot. Siddhant had spent a lifetime trying to live up to her expectations and follow her wishes, but the fact was that no matter how hard he tried, it was never enough for her. Over time, he had stopped trying to impress her. He simply listened to her wishes, and then did what he thought was right, regardless of whether it would please her or not.

'Well?' she prodded.

Siddhant took a deep breath and said in a calm voice, 'What do you want me to say? I know you want me to train under Dr Patel, but he's a neurosurgeon, and I need more time to decide if that's the route I want to take. For now, I think it's best if I learn everything, which is why I think Dr Mehta is the right fit for me. As a general surgeon, he can teach me a lot, and he actually likes me. We have a great professional relationship, and it's the one I want to build, for my career.'

'It sounds like your mind is made up.'

Siddhant sensed disappointment in her tone but he refused to dwell on it. 'Yes. Yes, it is,' he said finally.

'Fine, then do what you want. I can't believe you don't know what specialty you want to pursue yet. Your brother knew what he wanted to do from the very beginning.'

'Maa.' That's all Siddhant could say.

'I think that's enough,' his dad interjected sternly. 'People find their paths at their own pace, and we'd rather you took your time and made the choice that's right for you than jump into something rashly and regret it later.'

There was a silence, followed by some whispering.

'Agreed,' his mom relented.

After that, they asked him how he was doing, to which he responded vaguely. He knew full well that they didn't really want to know details; they were just fulfilling what they believed was an obligation. His mother didn't have a lot of patience for small talk and her agitation was thinly veiled; Siddhant could sense her eagerness to end the call. His mother was a brilliant woman and an accomplished surgeon, but she was seriously lacking in warmth and sensitivity – not what you want from your mother, but it came as no surprise to him. A lifetime of training had taught him to manage his expectations in order to not get his feelings hurt.

His parents had worked at AIIMS their entire careers, up until a few years ago, when they had moved to Germany to join a medical research project. They later invited Siddhant's older brother, Deepanshu, to join the project, but he was more interested in his surgical career and decided to stay in Delhi. Deepanshu eventually left AIIMS to join a private hospital in Mumbai. Siddhant suspected that he moved because he was trying to build a career separate from their parents', for which he couldn't blame Deepanshu.

By the time Siddhant got home, he had replayed the conversation with his parents in his mind many times more than prescribed. His head was bursting with retorts he came up with too late and now had to keep to himself. He felt far too agitated by this negative energy that was coursing through his veins.

When he walked into his bedroom, he was pleasantly surprised to find Akriti there. She was standing by the window, looking outside. A big smile appeared on Siddhant's face, and his pace quickened as he approached her.

'Oh, good. I'm so glad you're here tonight!' he said. He put his arms around her from behind and kissed her shoulder. 'You won't believe the conversation I just had with my parents. The things my mom said to me … It's stuff you would think about twice even before thinking it, but she just says it like it's nothing. And my dad just sits there and lets her bully me, like always. I thought things would change once they moved to Europe and there was some distance between us, but nope. I'm still just as much of a disappointment. I wish I hadn't taken his call in the first place.'

Akriti suddenly pushed Siddhant away, taking him by surprise. She spun around to look at him, her eyebrows arched in fury, as if he had just committed an unforgivable crime.

'What's going on?' he asked, completely baffled by her reaction.

'How can you say that? To me, of all people!' Akriti asked venomously.

'Say what? What did I say to make you so mad …?'

'I would give *anything* to talk to my dad again.' Akriti's voice was cold. She hid her face in her hands and turned away from Siddhant. 'Just once … if I could talk to him just once …'

Siddhant stood frozen on his spot, retracing his words. He'd been complaining about his parents, and he said he wished he hadn't taken his dad's call … The moment he realized what he'd done wrong, his face became warm with embarrassment.

'Crap, I'm sorry,' he said hurriedly. 'That was very insensitive of me. I didn't think about … I'm so sorry. That was super dumb of me.' He tried to hold her but Akriti pushed him away.

'Don't act all cute with me now. I'm serious.'

'I am too! I really am sorry I was so insensitive. I shouldn't have said that.'

For the second time that evening Siddhant felt like a child who had just been reproached. He stared at the back of Akriti's head and waited for her to say something.

'It's okay,' Akriti said finally, in a quiet voice.

'It was an honest mistake.'

'I know. It's okay.'

Siddhant squeezed her hand, and she let him, which he took as a good sign. 'Tell you what – let's go out, get a drink. I've had a long day, and we've been spending too much time cooped up inside. Let's go out for a couple of hours, get out of our own heads. What do you say?'

'I don't feel like going out …'

'Oh, come on! It'll be a nice change. We'll have fun, I promise,' Siddhant insisted. 'Please? Just for one drink?'

'You just don't get it, do you?' Akriti spat, the venom returning in her tone. 'I'm not in the *fun* kind of mood right now. God, you're so completely clueless sometimes. You can't just come in and say all that – and then make everything okay just by apologizing and getting a drink. That's not how it works. I'm not a robot.'

With that, Akriti grabbed her handbag from his bed and stormed out. Siddhant, who was too shocked to protest, watched her slam the door behind her, feeling worse than he had all day.

Chapter 6

Siddhant tapped his fingers on the steering wheel, absently humming the theme song of *Game of Thrones*. He had only been waiting ten minutes, but he was beginning to perspire – not the best start to the evening, which involved socializing with Akriti's friends at a loud, sweaty bar in Hauz Khas Village. He turned the AC on and picked up his phone.

He wanted to ask Akriti how much longer she would be, but didn't, worried that he might end up annoying her. He'd been on thin ice around her the past week; sometimes his mere existence seemed to annoy her. He wished he had a clue as to what he had done wrong, but asking her made her even madder, so he refrained.

After ten more minutes of waiting in the car, Siddhant saw Akriti finally emerge from her building. She was wearing a straight, long dress that was either black or a shade of navy so dark that it looked black under the dim street light. He got out of the car to greet her.

'You look very pretty,' Siddhant said, smiling warmly.

She allowed him a hug and half a smile before making her way to the passenger seat, her feathery earrings dangling all the way down to her shoulders. Siddhant got back in the car and pulled out of the parking.

The atmosphere in the car was tense. If he hadn't had such a great day at the hospital, he would've been more bothered by Akriti's sour mood. But given that he'd worked on three very perfectly executed surgeries in the past twelve hours, he had adrenaline rushing through his veins, keeping him buoyant.

'So, catch me up – you said it's your friend Smriti's birthday?' Siddhant asked.

'Yes.'

'And you know her from …?'

'School.'

'Okay. Is there going to be anyone there that I know?' Siddhant asked, bearing the weight of this one-sided conversation.

'Ashok.'

'Ashok,' Siddhant muttered, thinking about it. 'Doesn't trigger anything … Can you remind me?'

Akriti pursed her lips and sighed loudly, as if he was the dumbest person on the planet. 'He came by the hospital once? He was there to visit a friend but dropped by to say hi to us?'

'Oh, right. I remember now. In the cafeteria,' Siddhant said.

'Yes. Ashok is Smriti's boyfriend, so he's going to be there for sure. And then there are a bunch of people you'll be meeting for the first time. It's about time,' Akriti said.

Siddhant didn't read much into her last comment, and said instead, 'Great! I'm excited to meet your friends.'

They spent the rest of their drive listening to music ranging from bad to obscene. Frustrated by the quality of the music, Akriti kept changing the radio channels furiously. Siddhant stayed out of it. When they reached Hauz Khas Village at last, he was relieved not to have to witness the battle between Akriti and the radio channels any longer.

Weirdly enough, even though this unexpected and undesirable battle had somewhat dampened Siddhant's enthusiasm, he found comfort in the fact that Akriti's bad mood wasn't a result of something he had said or done. This was evidence that her general annoyance in life wasn't originating from him, so he shouldn't take it personally. Everybody had bad days, and since her bad day wasn't caused by him, he could try and make it better.

As they walked towards the Village from the parking lot, Siddhant racked his brain for something sweet he could do that would make her smile, or something funny that would make her laugh. Maybe at the bar, he could have the waiter bring out a special cocktail or dessert for her, with a note from him? That would be cute. She'd probably like that, unless she thought it was too cheesy in front of her friends. Hmm.

To begin with, he grabbed her hand as they walked towards the bar. Surprised, she glanced at him. He shot her a quick smile, but no sooner had he turned back towards the road than he immediately froze in his tracks.

Maahi.

Akriti stopped as well, looking up at him questioningly, but he barely registered anything. His brain refused to work. He couldn't bring his legs to move. He hadn't seen Maahi since they had broken up a year ago. She was wearing a very loose yellow t-shirt and jeans and had two cartons carefully tucked under her left arm.

He watched as Maahi stopped, readjusted the cartons under her arm and pulled out her phone from the back pocket of her jeans. She squeezed the phone between her ear and her right shoulder awkwardly and resumed walking. He heard her surprised 'What?' from a distance. His heart leapt to his throat. *He hadn't heard her voice in so long ...*

Their relationship had ended on reasonably good terms. There was no bad blood between them, and they had blamed everything on timing. By implication, things between them might have worked out in a different moment in time.

What they hadn't decided was whether they would remain friends and continue talking to each other. As it turned out, the night of their break-up was the last time they had seen each other ... until now.

In the past year, Siddhant had wondered, on occasion, if their paths would ever cross – since they lived in the same city – and how he would feel and behave if and when that happened. However, now that it had, his brain had been rendered completely useless.

'Sid?'

He heard Akriti's voice, as if through a fog, pulling him back to the present. What had seemed like years had in reality only been a few seconds – he could still recover from this, without making a complete fool of himself. He was caught off guard, that's all.

'Yes, sorry,' he mumbled and resumed walking, towing Akriti along with him.

'What's wrong?'

'It's nothing ...' He kept walking, feeling wildly unprepared to talk to Maahi again. He'd tried so hard for so long to forget about her.

'Someone you know?' she asked, her eyes darting from Siddhant to Maahi suspiciously.

There was no point trying to avoid the conversation. He knew Akriti enough to know that she wasn't going to let this go. 'Yes ... yeah, it's Maahi.'

Just as he said her name, Maahi turned towards them. For a second, her gaze went right past them, then returned to rest on Siddhant. As recognition settled in, her mouth opened slightly, and her eyes shifted to Akriti.

By then, Akriti had pulled Siddhant to her and they were standing face-to-face with Maahi.

'Call you in a bit,' Maahi said into her phone and shoved it back in her pocket. She smiled hesitantly. 'Hi, Siddhant.'

Her voice flooded him with a thousand memories that he tried to push away one by one. He pushed back the flurry of emotions rising within him and nodded mechanically. 'Hi, Maahi.'

It was a strange moment. Neither of them seemed to know what to do, so they just stood there, looking at each other. Maahi broke away first, her eyes lowering and falling on his hand, holding Akriti's. Then she looked away, half her face hiding behind her cap. Siddhant felt his entire body become warm. He couldn't process it; it was all so sudden. Akriti was clinging to him in ownership, Maahi looked thrown, he probably looked thrown too. Where do they go from here? What was he supposed to say?

'Hi,' Akriti said suddenly, brightly. 'I'm Akriti. Sid's girlfriend.'

'I'm Maahi. Nice to meet you,' she said evenly. He had to hand it to her – she looked unfazed, even warm, as she took Akriti's outstretched hand.

'So, what are you up to tonight?' Akriti asked, her voice more cheerful than he'd heard in a week. He felt sick. He didn't want to be a part of this, pretending that they were old friends.

'Just dropping off some inventory. We were short at this shop, so I brought some over from our other shop. We run a couple of bakeries, my friend and I,' Maahi explained to Akriti.

'Bakeries?' Akriti raised an eyebrow.

'Yes. We're called Cookies + Cupcakes. It's a – well, the name's self-explanatory.' Maahi laughed light-heartedly, glancing at Siddhant for a split second before fixing her gaze firmly on Akriti again.

'How *cute*!' Akriti sneered. 'Good for you.'

'Thanks. We love it.' A small frown appeared on Maahi's forehead, but she otherwise didn't reveal any sign of distress over Akriti's behaviour.

'I'm a neurosurgeon,' Akriti volunteered. Siddhant turned to look at Akriti, who continued, 'At AIIMS. With Siddhant – that's where we met. We're both surgical residents.'

'That's awesome,' Maahi said. A smile of genuine happiness stretched across her face as she looked at Siddhant. 'So, you found your calling, Siddhant? Neurosurgery?'

'Not exactly, not yet,' Siddhant said, remembering the countless conversations he'd had with Maahi about his interests and career path. 'It's a real possibility, but for now I'm still trying out a few different specialties.'

'But are you liking it? The residency?'

'Of course he is. We both are. It's *meaningful* work,' Akriti said pointedly, before Siddhant could respond. 'People don't become surgeons just by chance. And when you do something with deliberation and dedication – it pays off. Right, Sid?'

'Yes, Akriti, but I don't think Maahi was questioning that,' Siddhant said mildly. Their run-in was becoming increasingly uncomfortable.

'I just wanted to know how you were doing.' Maahi looked from Siddhant to Akriti, looking partly confused, partly suspicious.

'He's doing great,' Akriti said. She teamed her words with an ear to ear smile, looking up dreamily at Siddhant. She put an arm around him and placed the other hand on his chest.

Her open palm on his chest made Siddhant even more uncomfortable. Was it weird that the first time she was making physical contact like this with him was in front of his ex? That too when all day, she had barely said one kind word to him? 'I'm doing well,' he answered for himself. 'And yes, I'm liking the residency program. How have you been?'

'Good, good. We opened another store. Here in Hauz Khas.' Maahi motioned to the cartons she was holding as explanation. 'It's a lot of work, keeps us pretty busy, but we're not complaining.'

'Wow, congratulations on the new store. That's big!'

'Thanks, we're working on some very exciting projects, currently on the down low. I'm not sure I should start telling people yet … just keeping our fingers crossed.'

'Fair enough, I won't ask,' Siddhant said. 'How's Laila?'

'Awesome, as always! She's actually in Patna right now, visiting her family. So, extra work for me. Yay.' Maahi looked down at the cartons again.

'Okay … we'll let you carry on then,' Siddhant said, following her gaze.

'Yes, we have a party to go to, over at Mia Bella. We really must go,' Akriti said, checking her watch.

'That sounds fun.' Maahi smiled at them. 'It was nice seeing you guys.'

'Same here!' Akriti said.

Siddhant smiled back, not knowing what to do with himself. They had just spoken to each other as if they were mere acquaintances who had once gone to college together, or known each other vaguely through mutual friends. Nothing about Maahi's behaviour suggested that his sudden appearance had had any kind of emotional effect on her. Either she was good at hiding her feelings, or she genuinely wasn't affected. He hoped he'd come across as unaffected as her, even though that was miles from how he truly felt.

Maahi walked away from them, after shooting a final good-natured smile in their direction. He watched her for a second, before becoming aware of Akriti's eyes on him. There was nothing to do but let her drag him away, clinging to his arm like two people had never been more in love.

As soon as Maahi was out of sight, Akriti loosened her grip on Siddhant's arm and turned to him, saying quietly, 'She seemed nice.'

It was a statement, not a question, but Siddhant knew that he had to watch his response. 'Mm-hm,' he murmured noncommittally.

'Cookies and Cupcakes though.' Akriti laughed. 'Wow, I guess some people really don't look for meaning or fulfilment in their work, do they?'

Siddhant had a strong urge to respond to that, but he kept his mouth shut – not because of what he wanted to say, but because of who it was about. It would surely become a 'thing', and he didn't want to get into yet another thing with Akriti.

'Oh my God! You don't buy into it, do you?' Akriti persisted. 'Please tell me you don't think it's "aww, so cute" what she's doing!'

'I don't think that's her intention,' Siddhant said finally.

'Really? So, you're saying that's her true passion? The thing she's best at in life?'

'Akriti, stop.'

'No, seriously? Baking cookies? *That's* her special talent?' Akriti smirked.

'Undermining someone's work isn't my style,' Siddhant said firmly, choosing his words very carefully. 'Different things make different people happy, and I'm not one to judge someone else for their passion. You know too little about Maahi to pass any kind of judgement.'

'Wow. Are you serious right now? You're taking your ex-girlfriend's side?' Akriti rounded on him, as if he'd said something utterly absurd. They were standing at the bottom of the staircase leading to the bar.

'I'm not taking any sides! I'm simply saying that we shouldn't be bothered by someone else's profession. How does it affect us, in any way at all?'

'But why does it bother you so much if I talk about her—?'

'It's not about her. No work is small, and judging people by their choice of profession is not something I'm interested in. That's all I'm saying.' Siddhant stood his ground. He saw a few people approaching them purposefully. 'Are they your friends?' he asked, lowering his voice.

'What?' Akriti asked, turning around to look at them. 'Yes.' She added in an angry whisper, 'You're a surgeon for God's sake! How can you even say with a straight face that baking is as important as—?'

'Can we please drop this?' Siddhant said. 'Your friends are here.'

Within seconds, Akriti's friends were greeting them with handshakes and hugs, which put enough distance between the two of them to prevent the conversation from continuing. Siddhant was grateful, but he wasn't fooled for one second – this wasn't the last of it.

And sure enough, Akriti spent the rest of the evening aloof and distant from him. This put Siddhant in an awkward position, since she was the only person he knew there. She wasn't outright mean to him in front of her friends, but he essentially spent the evening very aware of how displeased she was with him.

He contemplated for a second if he wanted to do the special flower or dessert thing for her, but he suspected that it would not only be a wasted effort, but she would also take it as an apology or an admission of guilt on his part, and that will become a whole another thing he didn't want to deal with.

Instead, he let Akriti fume. For the first time, he didn't care that he was making her unhappy. She was clearly in the wrong. Maahi had been nothing but pleasant to them in what Akriti was intent on making a very unpleasant encounter for all of them. He also didn't like how she had placed her hand on his chest or how she was clinging to him when they walked away – neither of those things were natural to them, or something they'd ever done before. Akriti had used him, in whatever ego game she had been playing with Maahi, and he didn't appreciate that kind of treatment. He also had no interest in putting on a show to hurt others or prove a false point.

And Maahi … Siddhant tried not to think about her. Their meeting had been so sudden, and had ended so fast – he was still reeling in its impact. He put it out of his mind as he smiled at something one of Akriti's friends said. But no matter how hard he tried, there was one thing he couldn't forget – the look in Maahi's eyes when she saw Akriti's hand on his chest.

It was only there for a second, that look of pain. But then it was gone, to be replaced by a friendly, carefully plastered smile. Was he sure it was pain? Could it just be surprise, shock or embarrassment because he caught her looking, or something else? Maybe he'd imagined it altogether.

Chapter 7

Siddhant didn't have to wait long to find out how Akriti felt about their run-in with Maahi. After spending an entire evening appearing stand-offish, drinking too much and shooting Siddhant hurt glances as if *he* was the reason behind all her unhappiness, Akriti asked him about Maahi as soon as they parted ways from her friends and got in the car.

'When were you going to tell me about her?'

Siddhant was in no mood to discount her behaviour. 'Fasten your seat belt, please,' he said in a quiet voice.

Akriti ignored his request and continued, 'Answer me.'

'I won't start the car until you fasten your seat belt.'

'Were you ever going to tell me about her?'

'Tell you *what* about her?' Siddhant bit.

'About her *existence*, to begin with.'

'I didn't think you'd expect me to never have been in a relationship before you.'

'That's not the point! *You didn't tell me*, you hid it from me. Why did you do that?' Akriti was looking at him accusingly.

'I didn't hide anything from you. We just haven't really … got to that point yet,' Siddhant said evenly, determined to have a rational conversation. 'We haven't got to the point of discussing exes and past relationships.'

'Why? What are we waiting for?'

'Nothing! I just don't think it's the best topic of conversation right in the beginning of a new relationship. I know it feels like longer, but you and I only went on our first date, what, three months ago? Shouldn't this phase be about us – you and me, spending time together, getting to know each other? And not about relationships we've had in the past that failed? What is the point of talking about that?'

'Stop trying to change the topic,' Akriti snapped, refusing to acknowledge anything he was saying.

'How am I changing the topic?' Siddhant said, trying very hard to remain calm. 'I'm addressing the very question you asked. You asked me why I didn't say anything about Maahi, and I'm telling you why. Do you really want to talk about my past relationships now when we could be spending time with each other in the present? We've already wasted this whole night instead of enjoying each other's company ...'

'Again, with the ... round and round. Stop – stop trying to confuse me ...'

'I'm not trying to do that!'

'Then tell me about her!' Akriti burst out, now looking positively panicked. 'You're saying all these words, but you still won't talk about her. Why won't you tell me about her?'

She was looking at him pleadingly, and he found himself cornered. Siddhant didn't want to talk about Maahi – to anyone, and especially not to Akriti. Ever since Maahi and he broke up, he'd tried very hard not to think about her.

Even though they had ended things on reasonably good terms, there was a lot there that had been left unresolved. They had been together, deliriously in love … until one day it all fell apart. And for no fault of his, he couldn't be with her anymore. The decision to break up was one they'd made together, because no matter how much they loved each other, there were things that had happened, an incident that couldn't be undone … and it hurt too much to be together.

Siddhant had been careful never to question whether it hurt him more *not* to be with Maahi … because he wasn't sure he would like the answer. So, he'd done his very best not to think about her, rely on distractions and keep on breathing.

Akriti was watching him, calmer now.

'What do you want to know?' Siddhant asked quietly.

'How did you meet her?'

'At a coffee shop. I used to go there after my shifts at the hospital. She was a barista there.'

'Barista? But she said she's a baker.'

'She started out as a barista. She discovered that she wanted to be a baker while working at that coffee shop. Then she started her own bakery.'

'How often would you go there to see her?'

'Akriti, stop,' Siddhant said firmly. He reached for her hand and held it in both his. 'What's the point of talking about all this?'

'I want to know.' Akriti was adamant. She let him hold her hand, but remained undeterred from her mission. 'When was this?'

'A couple of years ago. Back when I was doing my internship at AIIMS.'

'How long were you with her?'

'A year or so.'

'Who broke up with whom?'

'It was mutual,' Siddhant said after a moment.

'It's never mutual.' Akriti snorted.

'It was. I don't know how to explain it – I guess we both knew it had to end and agreed that that was the only option we had. The timing wasn't right for us.'

'Did she dump you? You can just tell me.'

'She didn't …' Siddhant paused. 'Fine, if you really must know – something happened, and we both knew that because of that, I had to end it. I didn't have to actually do it, because she realized what had to happen too. She didn't try to stop me. We both knew time was not on our side.'

'That's it? You never had an actual conversation with each other? You didn't even *say* you were breaking up?'

'We didn't argue or anything, no. It's complicated. We did have a conversation, but the break-up was more in the subtext. Both of us knew that we had broken up. We didn't … linger, because there was no point. I … I don't know how to explain it.'

Siddhant felt a weight at the bottom of his stomach. He remembered that night very clearly. As soon as he found out what had happened, he knew they were over. Yet, they couldn't come to terms with it immediately. It was so sudden, so heart-breaking. He'd felt so lost, as though he was missing a part of himself. The only way he could recover was by pretending that he was okay, nothing was wrong, things were as normal as they could be – delusion was his only option. He couldn't accept the loss, or handle the mourning that came with it.

'What happened?' Akriti's voice broke into his thoughts.

'Hmm?'

'You said something happened that made you both realize that breaking up was the only option. What happened?'

Siddhant met Akriti's eyes. She seemed to have sobered up significantly during the course of their conversation. 'She hadn't … fully resolved her issues with her ex-boyfriend, and then he suddenly reappeared in her life. They had had a bad break-up and I guess some … feelings were still there, and his sudden reappearance in her life threw things off balance. Like I said, the timing didn't work for us—'

'She cheated on you?'

'No!' Siddhant protested involuntarily. 'No, I mean … they kissed … there was a kiss, but it wasn't like that. It was a complicated situation. It wasn't deliberate – they weren't having an affair behind my back or anything. She didn't plan for it to happen—'

'Why are you defending her?' Akriti swiftly pulled her hand out of his and tilted her head to the side questioningly.

'I'm not defending her. I'm telling you the truth.'

'Sounds to me like she cheated on you!'

'Akriti, stop. Please. Can we not do this anymore? I've told you everything you wanted to know. Can we go home now?' Siddhant pleaded. It was past 2 a.m., and he was getting really tired of this conversation. He hadn't even had the chance to process the unexpected encounter with Maahi. The last thing he wanted to do was talk to Akriti about her and evaluate why that relationship had crumbled. There was no scenario in which talking to Akriti about Maahi could end well.

Unfortunately, Akriti was in no mood to let it go. 'Why won't you admit that she cheated on you?'

'Akriti, I've told you so many times now – I don't want to talk about this anymore,' Siddhant said firmly.

'But I do!'

'Fasten your seatbelt. We can't sit in this parking lot forever.'

'When did you guys break up?'

'Akriti, we need to go. Can you please fasten your seatbelt?'

'No, you can't ignore my questions. Answer me!'

'Fine. We broke up about a year ago. Happy?' Siddhant said, now thoroughly frustrated with her and the situation.

'Did you decide to remain friends? Did you stay in touch?'

'No.'

'You didn't see her at all after you broke up?'

'No.'

'Until tonight?'

'Yes.'

'Are you serious?'

'Yes! Can we stop now? I don't understand how this is the right time or place to have this conversation, or why we need to have this conversation at all.' Siddhant let his head fall back on the head-rest of his seat and closed his eyes.

'Because you didn't tell me about her till I met her. Do you have any idea how that felt? Being in the dark like that?'

'It never came up. We've never talked about exes—'

'We would've, if I had known that there was some girl you used to be in love with, right here in Delhi, who you are still defending for some reason!' Akriti's voice was getting louder, her anger returning.

'I'm not defend—' Siddhant was utterly exhausted. 'Fine. Fine, she cheated on me. We broke up. I hadn't seen or spoken to her until tonight. Okay? Can we move on now, please?'

'I don't understand why it bothers you so much to talk about her … Are you not over her? Do you still have feelings—?'

'Oh God, seriously?' Siddhant ran his fingers through his hair. 'Can we just stop now? We don't need to talk about any of this—'

'Why not?'

'Because there's nothing to talk about! It's all in the past. I don't think about any of it anymore, it shouldn't affect our lives and I don't want to talk about it,' Siddhant said with finality.

'And what I want doesn't even matter?' Akriti challenged.

'What are you talking about?! We've been doing exactly what *you* want all night – talking about my ex in the parking lot at 3 a.m. I'm so tired, Akriti. Let's please just go home.'

'No! I think it's really weird that you're avoiding this conversation—'

'How am I avoiding this conversation? We've *had* this conversation. We've been having it all night and now it's over. I can't do this anymore.' Siddhant sighed loudly, feeling trapped in the car, in his own skin. He had a strong urge to punch something, to just get out and run.

Akriti didn't say anything. She turned away from him and sat back, looking out of the window. Then, after a minute, she pulled on her seat belt and fastened it around herself.

Siddhant turned the key in the ignition and pulled out of the parking lot. His thoughts and the conversation he'd had with Akriti muddled his head. He could make neither head nor tail of it. He was unable to process all that had happened that night, where it started and where it ended or what it would mean to him when he woke up the next morning. Would Akriti still be mad at him? He couldn't worry about that – for now, it was over.

❦

It wasn't over.

When Siddhant stopped outside her building, Akriti didn't get out of the car. She had fallen asleep, her head against the window. She took a moment to wake up fully and regain her bearings. Then she looked at Siddhant, with the saddest expression on her face.

'Sid,' she said, her lower lip trembling.

'Yes.'

'She's so pretty.'

'Akriti, please. Please, let it go,' Siddhant begged. 'We broke up a year ago. I didn't expect to see her, or I would've told you about her. I'm sorry I hurt you.'

'You said it was the timing ...' It was as if Akriti hadn't heard anything he said.

'What?'

'You said it wasn't the right time for the two of you. She wasn't over her ex and made a mistake ...' Akriti said, her voice breaking. 'What if that's changed now? What if now the timing is right?'

'It isn't! How can the timing be right now, when I'm in a relationship? With you! For all we know, she might be with someone too. We have completely different lives now, lives that practically never intersect,' Siddhant declared, a tightness forming in his throat as he said those words.

'But if the timing was right now ... would you choose her over me?' Akriti asked in a small voice.

'Are you listening to me—?'

'I'm dark. And defective—' she continued gravely.

'What—?'

'She's pretty and perfect. She bakes cookies. Her bed is probably made of rainbows and butterflies. Does she have a pet unicorn?' she finished bitterly.

What is happening? Siddhant was completely baffled by the nosedive this conversation had taken. Granted, he had only known Akriti for three months, but he had never seen her so insecure before.

He also disapproved of her assumption that Maahi's life was easy, and she didn't have any real problems because of her choice of profession. It was unfair and judgemental of Akriti to think like that and be dismissive of Maahi's profession. Siddhant thought it cast Akriti in a very bad light. She was a hardworking surgeon; she shouldn't feel the need to judge others and put them down to feel better about herself.

Siddhant had no idea how to tackle this situation. He wanted to comfort her and make her feel better. Yet, at the same time, he didn't want her to think it was okay to have accusatory conversations like this with him or bully others.

'That's enough, Akriti. You have to stop,' Siddhant said finally.

'Why did you say we weren't at the point of discussing past relationships?'

'What?' Siddhant was thrown again. She wasn't listening to a word he was saying. It was like she was having a conversation with herself.

'Aren't you serious about me?'

'I don't know what the right answer is here. What do you want me to say?'

'You're not! You're just playing with me!' Fat teardrops began rolling down her face, as if on cue.

'What—no! I care about you!'

'You said you love me!'

'I did! I do!'

'You're lying. You're a liar! Akriti spat angrily. She wiped her cheek with the back of her hand. 'You're a liar!'

'Stop it! I'm not a liar! I have never lied to you,' Siddhant said desperately. The situation was spinning out of control again and like before, he had no idea how to fix it.

'You don't love me!'

Siddhant paused for a breath and picked his words carefully. 'I told you I love you. It was true then and it is true now. But it is also true that we have only known each other for three months. Love takes time. I'm getting to know you better each day. It takes time for two people to develop a deep connection. We can't expect to fall madly in love overnight, that our love will be as strong as that of a couple who have been together for fifty years!'

'So what are you saying?'

'I'm saying that ... why are we putting so much pressure on ourselves, and our relationship? Can we just stop worrying about things that don't affect us and live in the present?'

'So now I'm putting pressure on you? What are you talking about?' Akriti's voice was getting high-pitched again, and even though she'd stopped crying, the hurt look had reappeared in her eyes.

'No! God!' Siddhant rubbed his hands over his face in frustration. 'I'm just saying that we don't need to put a label on our relationship and follow some sort of manual. We should just focus on getting to know each other, and allowing ourselves to—'

'What kind of bullshit is this? What a fucking joke—'

'Akriti! This conversation is going nowhere—'

'Because you're just bullshitting me—'

'Stop it!' Siddhant said loudly, overpowering Akriti's cries. 'Just STOP!'

Taken aback, Akriti turned quiet immediately. Then in the next second she jumped out of the car and stormed into her building.

Siddhant didn't go after her. There was no point trying to reason with her in her current state. They both needed to sleep it off. Every word that came out of her made less sense than the last and nothing he said was making any difference at all. They were just going around in circles, and by that point he was so dizzy he couldn't tell which side was up.

He had to let her go for now, give her time to cool down. Most of all, he felt tired to the bone and just wanted to go home.

Chapter 8

Over the next week, Siddhant and Akriti circled each other much like wrestlers gauging their opponent before a match. They tried to assess where the other person was, emotionally, and how to move on from the night at the parking lot.

They didn't text or make any plans to hang out. When they saw each other at the hospital, the most one offered the other was a swift nod or a hesitant smile. Neither of them was sure about how to recover from their fight.

Siddhant thought putting some space between them was the best idea; they needed time to process things. Besides, he was in no rush to make up with her. She had been unreasonable, irrational, suspicious and distrusting of him – and for no real reason as far as he could see. He might have reconciled with her behaviour if she had stopped after the first few questions. But getting drunk and picking a fight ...

By the time he'd returned home that night, he had a splitting headache. Yet, he couldn't sleep. He lay awake in his bed for hours, going over everything she'd said to him. Since he'd known he would be driving after the party, he had refrained from drinking – which meant once he fell into bed, he didn't even have the luxury of simply passing out.

He'd arrived at work with just a couple of hours of sleep, resulting in a day that was far more tiring than usual. He barely made it through their morning rounds, constantly stifling yawns. He finally saw Akriti when he got out of his first surgery of the day. She was talking to two people; the three of them huddled together in a group. She looked at him as he walked by. The only reaction he got from her in those few seconds was a startled expression. The following day, she gave him a nod as a hello.

A week later, they were yet to exchange more than cursory acknowledgements in the corridors. Siddhant was growing tired of the situation and wanted things to go back to normal, but he didn't know how to make that happen. He also believed that he deserved an apology from her, for treating him the way she had that night. Although he wasn't angry anymore – it wasn't in his nature to hold grudges – he did think that she ought to be the one to initiate conversation.

✿

A few days later, Siddhant got home from work to find Akriti in his living room. She was wearing a flowing blue kurti and had tied the top half of her hair in a really high ponytail at the crown of her head. When she turned to look at him, her bright pink lips stretched in a big smile.

'Hey, Sid!' she greeted cheerfully.

Siddhant looked back at his front door, wondering if he'd entered another dimension. Last time he'd checked, his life didn't look like this. Ever since Akriti had entered his life, he had become incapable of gauging what the next day would be like. At the moment, it looked like a scene from a romantic comedy.

'What's going on?' he wondered aloud as he set his bag down on the floor.

Akriti produced a long-stemmed white rose from behind her as she came towards him. Handing it to him, she leaned in and kissed him on the cheek. When she pulled back, she was looking at him with pure adoration. She smiled and returned to the table she'd been setting. 'I just wanted to do something special for you,' she explained.

Siddhant stood there, holding the white rose, which he now understood to be a signal of peace. Is this how they were going to make up? Brush everything under the rug and ignore the important conversations? Just pretend everything was ... rosy?

He set the rose on the kitchen counter and walked to the table. The table, covered with a pale pink cloth, was set for two. Each setting had a cloth napkin, rolled up and fastened with a wide gold ring, placed on a small plate, which was then placed on top of a large plate. To the right of each plate sat a knife and spoon and to the left were three forks of varying sizes – more than he'd ever used for one meal in his life. There were three little orange tea lights in the centre of the table. There were three glasses per person too, which he found confusing.

'Wow.' Siddhant wondered how long it had taken Akriti to put all of it together. He'd never seen anything like it before.

'Do you like it?' she asked eagerly.

'Like it? This is … Wow! I've never seen anything like this, at least not in person,' Siddhant said honestly.

Akriti laughed. 'Yeah, I got inspiration from Pinterest.'

'What are all these forks for?'

'They each have a purpose! My mom taught me how to use five-piece cutlery when I was young. We used to host a lot of parties, because her work required a lot of socializing and stuff.'

'Great – then you can teach me,' Siddhant said. 'It'll be like the how-to-be-a-proper-lady etiquette training they used to have in Britain.'

'Almost exactly like that, yes.'

'And then I can sit pretty and wait for suitors to line up for me?' Siddhant asked in all seriousness.

'Pretty much,' Akriti responded swiftly.

'Sweet!'

They both laughed, and the tension between them broke. Maybe this wasn't how Siddhant would've chosen to resolve their fight – maybe he would've preferred to acknowledge the things that were said and feelings that were hurt in the process. But pushing it all under the rug felt so good … For once he was okay with taking the easy way out.

Akriti had, after all, put in a lot of effort to set this up. The least he could do was go along with it.

The doorbell rang and Akriti sprang into action at once. 'That's our food,' she said, going towards the door. She came back to the table carrying a large paper bag.

As they began extracting boxes from the bag, Siddhant asked, 'What are we having?'

'Italian,' Akriti said, looking up at him with a twinkle in her eyes.

'Oh, cool.' Siddhant felt like he was missing something.

'Just like our first date,' Akriti explained. 'Don't you remember? I thought it's your favourite.' She looked at him quizzically.

'Yes, of course. I love it!' Siddhant said, biting his lip.

Akriti visibly relaxed and brought out the remaining boxes. Siddhant didn't correct her – they did get Italian food on their first date, but not because it was his favourite. It was because he had asked her what she was in the mood for and then picked out the restaurant based on her response. But pretending that Italian food was his favourite was a small price to pay for some peace between them.

'Let me wash up quickly and come back,' Siddhant said.

'Don't be long!' Akriti smiled. As he walked away, she added, 'Food's getting cold.'

'Just a second,' Siddhant called from the door to the bathroom. He saw his reflection in the mirror and was disappointed to find a tired face looking back at him. His hair was going in five different directions and badly needed a cut. His facial hair could do with some trimming too. He hadn't had time to shave for over a week, resulting in a full face of beard and moustache. He pulled his T-shirt over his head and bent down to wash his face. He tried to fix his hair, and was successful in taming part of it. Buttoning down a fresh shirt, he peeked under his bed and pulled out two bottles and took them to the living room.

'White or red?' he asked Akriti, holding up the wine bottles. 'Found some leftover bottles from a party we had a while ago.'

'Red would be lovely,' Akriti said, still pretending to be in a rom-com.

Siddhant smiled, thinking about how hard she was trying to make everything perfect, and uncorked the wine bottle. They sat down across from each other and he poured her a glass. She waited till he had poured himself some, and then raised her glass.

'To a beautiful night,' Akriti said, smiling lovingly at him.

'To a beautiful night,' Siddhant repeated. He took a sip and looked down at the table in front of him, completely blown away. It looked even more appealing now, with the food and wine adorning it. 'So, which fork should I use for the pasta?'

Akriti motioned towards a fork. 'This one. But I promise I won't judge you if you use the wrong one. This is a safe place!'

'Really? What if I eat with a spoon?'

'That's okay too.'

'What if I eat with my fingers? I can make them look like prongs of a giant fork …' Siddhant teased.

'Go ahead!' Akriti laughed.

'Wow. I'll be honest with you – I expected more strictness from my how-to-be-a-proper-lady teacher. What if suitors don't line up outside my door tomorrow?'

'Good for me! I get to keep you.' Akriti grinned at Siddhant.

'Ah, you have ulterior motives – now it all makes sense!' Siddhant shook his head in mock disappointment. 'Pure evil.'

'Hey, I'm just trying to keep my man, you can't blame me!' Akriti reached out and took Siddhant's hand.

As the meal progressed, Siddhant forgot all about their horrible fight, that awful night that had dragged on for hours. Akriti was going out of her way to make the moment special for them, and he appreciated all of it. Halfway through their meal, Priyesh returned from work. When he saw the romantic-candle-lit-dinner-for-two arrangements in the living room, he went straight to his bedroom and made himself scarce.

'Should we ask him to join us?' Siddhant suggested in a low voice.

'Here?' Akriti asked, completely confused by his question.

Siddhant immediately backtracked. 'No, of course not. This is for us. Never mind.'

'I guess we can, if you want to …'

'No, no. We'll let him know afterwards that we have more food if he wants …'

'Okay,' Akriti said, pursing her lips.

'I'm sorry,' Siddhant said proactively. 'You've put so much thought and effort into making this a special date for us. It was stupid of me to suggest that.'

Akriti smiled at him. 'Thank you for understanding.'

Although relieved, Siddhant could tell that the mood had shifted – it wasn't as relaxed as it had been just a few moments ago. He immediately began thinking of ways to change that.

'What's your day like tomorrow? If you don't have an early start, would you like to stay here tonight? We can watch a movie, or start a TV series together?' Siddhant suggested, racking his brains and coming up with one clichéd idea after another. 'Or we could play … Never mind, that's dumb.'

'Play?' Akriti raised an eyebrow.

'I meant video games. It's stupid – forget I suggested that,' Siddhant said. Looking at Akriti sitting across from him, he couldn't think of anyone less likely to be interested in playing video games with him.

'Ah … I thought you meant play, as in *play*.' She winked at him, then burst out laughing.

Siddhant joined her, thinking it was a joke, until the next moment – when Akriti dabbed her lips on her napkin and got up. She held his hand and tugged to make him get up. Once he got to his feet, she pulled him into his bedroom. Siddhant simply followed, too surprised to do anything else.

Akriti shut the door and then pushed Siddhant up against it. Her eyes holding his, she took three steps back, stopped, brought her hands behind her neck and undid the strap holding her outfit up. As the garment fell to the floor, Siddhant gulped, realizing two things. One, what he had thought was a long kurti was actually a dress, and two, Akriti was wearing lacy purple lingerie underneath – a nearly transparent bodysuit that started right above her breasts and ended at the top of her legs.

'Akriti.' Her name came out of Siddhant's mouth involuntarily.

'Yes, baby,' Akriti whispered, walking back to him. She reached up and kissed him, lingeringly, her palms placed firmly against his chest for support.

Siddhant snaked his arm around her waist and pulled her closer. He tilted his head to one side and slid his free hand behind her neck. He let it rest there, just below her ear, cradling her chin as he kissed her.

When he opened his eyes a few seconds later, he found Akriti watching him. He smiled at her, between kisses, and she broke away.

Leaving a trail of kisses from his lips to his ear, she whispered, 'Do you like it?'

'This?' he asked, his eyes travelling down her lace-clad body.

'Yes …'

'I was a little surprised, to be honest,' Siddhant let out a nervous laugh, caressing her lower back over the lace.

'What do you mean?' Akriti cocked her head to one side.

'Just that this is a little unexpected.' Siddhant's heartbeat quickened for all the wrong reasons. He had a feeling that if he didn't control the situation quickly, it was likely to tumble south. 'I didn't think we were there yet, that's all,' he explained softly.

'Why not? Didn't you say you love me? And I love you. What else do we need? What are we waiting for?' Akriti challenged him. 'And *don't* say this is getting to know each other better!' she added before he could respond.

'I wasn't going to! If anything, I think this is a fun part of getting to know each other,' Siddhant said. 'I didn't mean—'

'You never mean anything, do you?' Akriti pulled back from him forcefully and bent down to grab her dress. Covering herself with it, she said, 'Why do you have to be like this? What is wrong with you, Sid? Why do you have to complicate everything? I planned this special night for us. I wanted everything between us to be perfect – from the white rose to this lingerie. I thought tonight was going to be amazing—'

'And it is!' Siddhant said desperately. 'I only said that I was surprised, that's all!'

Akriti went on as if he hadn't spoken at all. 'Look at me!' She threw away the dress she was holding up against her body and demanded. 'Do you know what it takes for a girl to bare herself in front of someone like this? I only did it because I love you!'

Siddhant picked up her dress from the floor and handed it to her. He spoke hurriedly. 'Akriti, please try to understand. I do appreciate everything, really—'

'No, you *don't*! I do all of this for you, go out of my way to please you …' Akriti snatched her dress from him and cried, 'And what do you do? Make me feel like … like some common whore!'

'What? No! What are you …?' Siddhant had no words. Flabbergasted, he stood there as she got her stuff together and stormed out of his room. He followed her, pleading, 'I'm so sorry if I made you feel ... Akriti, please listen to me ...'

Akriti grabbed her handbag and keys, her back turned to Siddhant. 'Don't even bother.'

'Please, no – you're misunderstanding me ...' He tried to take her hand, but she jerked it away.

'Let me go! I don't want to be here anymore.'

'You don't have to stay here if you don't want to, but at least let me drive you. You've had wine ...'

'Oh, grow up! I had one glass, maybe two. Don't start pretending to care about me now!' Akriti snapped, and before he could say another word, she left.

✿

A few minutes later when Priyesh tiptoed out of his bedroom, Siddhant was still frozen to the spot where Akriti had left him. He looked at Priyesh, whose expression clearly gave away that he'd heard something.

'What did you do?' Priyesh asked.

'I ... really don't know.'

Priyesh nodded thoughtfully. 'Did you ask her?'

'She seemed to know, but it didn't make sense to me.' Siddhant shook his head, hoping something would rattle inside, help him make sense of the tornado that just hit his relationship.

'She sounded really pissed,' Priyesh observed.

'I know.'

'Even slammed the door and everything.'

'I know.'

'What are you gonna do?'

'I don't know.'

'Ooh, is there food?' Priyesh asked, sniffing.

'Have at it,' Siddhant waved towards the leftovers and walked to his bedroom in a daze, his brain working overtime to process this new plot twist.

Chapter 9

The next morning when Siddhant went to work, it was with a plan to be proactive about the situation with Akriti. He wasn't going to let this go on for days or weeks this time. He would find her and apologize for the way things had unravelled the night before. He was unsure as to what had happened, and what his part was in it all, but he knew that he'd hurt her and owed her an apology.

Unfortunately, by the time he located her, she had already started rounds. Soon after, he was pulled into his own work, and didn't come up for air until later in the evening. When he found out from Prachi that Akriti had already left work, he headed over to her place as soon as he was done for the day.

Akriti opened the door with a stoic expression on her face. She moved aside to let him in, but she didn't actually look at him. Even after she'd shut the door behind her, she didn't move. Her gaze was fixed on the rug on her living room floor.

'Are you okay …?' Siddhant asked, trying to meet her eyes.

Akriti shrugged, still refusing to look up.

'Akriti, I need to say something to you,' Siddhant began. Although she showed no signs of having heard him, he continued, 'I know I messed up. And I'm so sorry about that. The way things went down last night ... I regret it. It took me a minute to realize what was happening. I was surprised – but in a good way. In a very good way, in fact! I never meant to imply anything else, or make you feel bad, or ... cheap. I know how much courage it took for you to be so vulnerable in front of me. I'm so sorry that I didn't have the right words last night, and that I ended up hurting you. But you have to know how much I regret it. And I promise I will be more sensitive from now and watch the stupid words that come out of my mouth.'

He paused, trying to figure out her reaction. She hadn't moved or looked up even once.

'So, bottom line, I'm very sorry. I feel terrible about last night and I promise I'll be better in the future,' Siddhant said, approaching her.

He warily tried to hold her hand. And to his surprise, she let him. Emboldened by this small indication, Siddhant hooked his finger under her chin and lifted her face to his. Her eyes were brimming with tears. She looked down, causing the tears in her eyes to escape and flow down her cheeks.

'Hey! Please don't cry,' Siddhant said. He put his arms around her and pulled her close to him. Bending down to kiss her head, he muttered in her hair, 'I'm really, really sorry. I know it was a big deal. We've never really done anything physical before ... and it was the first time we were making out, and I messed up. I'm so stupid, and so, so sorry. Please don't cry.'

Akriti shook her head under his chin.

'I don't know how to help you,' Siddhant said helplessly.

Akriti pulled away from him, placing her palms against his chest. She stood there, holding him at an arm's length, her body convulsed with sobs.

'Akriti, please …' Siddhant begged. He hated to think that he had somehow caused her so much pain, and grappled with finding a way to rectify his mistake. 'What can I do? I was insensitive—'

'No, I don't care about that,' Akriti cut him off, shaking her head, her face crumpled.

'You don't care?' Siddhant asked, a little hurt. So much for the carefully thought-out monologue he'd practised in front of the mirror that morning. He pushed aside his own hurt feelings and focussed on the situation at hand. 'What's going on then? What happened?' *What more could've happened between the time she left his place last night and now to make her this upset?*

'What do you mean what happened?' Akriti said, her hands dropping from his chest. 'You don't know what's wrong?'

'I thought you were mad about last night—'

'Oh, get over yourself! Not everything is about you.'

'I didn't mean that—'

'Did you honestly just forget *what happened*?' Akriti cried.

'Is this about—?'

'It has only been a few months since I lost my father! My only real family. Now I have no one. I'm absolutely fucking alone. No one gives a fuck.' Akriti slid to her knees.

Siddhant was crouching by her side the next second. 'You're not alone. Please don't think like that. I'm here. You're never alone,' he assured her fervently. He had foolishly assumed that she had slowly been getting better and hadn't seen this coming.

'But I am,' Akriti whimpered.

'Akriti, please. Don't say that! You're so loved and cared for,' Siddhant said earnestly.

'It doesn't matter! No one can replace him. He was my father. He raised me, took care of me from the day I was born till the day he died. He taught me everything I know. He was always there for me. No one can take his place!' Akriti cried, more sobs shaking her body. She was still kneeling on the floor, her face hidden in her hands.

Siddhant paused for a minute, measuring his words before saying them aloud; nothing he had said to Akriti of late had landed correctly. Even when he had the best intentions, he ended up upsetting her. 'I know that no one can replace your father. I never meant to imply that—'

All of a sudden, Akriti sat back on the floor. She sighed loudly, and then wiped her face with both her hands. 'I know that. I know you didn't,' she said finally.

'I just want you to know that you're not alone. And you're not unloved or uncared for,' Siddhant said solemnly.

'Thank you for saying that.'

'I'm not just saying it; I mean it.'

Akriti reached out and held his hand. There was such sadness in her eyes that Siddhant felt he would give every last thing he possessed just to get her to smile once. He hated to see her so sad, facing something so terrible every day. No matter how many times he told her that she wasn't alone, the fact was that even though he was by her side, despite his best efforts, he was failing to be much help.

'All I can tell you is that it'll get better with time. Right now, when you think of your dad, you only think about your loss, the tragedy – that's the main focus of your thoughts, and rightfully so. It's still very raw, and I'm sure … I cannot even imagine how hard it must be for you.' Siddhant paused, gathering his thoughts in order to come up with something helpful. 'But in time, you will be able to think of the good times you spent together, of the love you shared. And until then, I'm here for you. Whatever you need me for, count me in. If I can lessen your pain even by a small fraction, I'll do anything.'

'Sid, don't.' Akriti's lips were pursed tightly.

'Don't – what?'

'Don't be so sweet to me.'

'You can't stop me,' Siddhant said stubbornly.

Akriti let out a laugh in between sobs. 'You're going to force your sweetness on me?'

'If you don't accept it nicely.'

Akriti laughed again, but then quietened down in the next second. 'I'm so sorry, for everything.'

The sincerity in her eyes caught Siddhant off guard. She reminded him of the Akriti from their first date, from before the phone call about her dad, before everything went wrong. That girl didn't play games. She was honest, direct, no bullshit.

'You have nothing to apologize for,' Siddhant said.

'I do, and you know that.'

Siddhant was quiet.

'I know that I've been difficult to be around,' Akriti said. 'I see what's happening … when it's happening. I don't know how to explain it. When I'm arguing with you, I know what I'm doing, and I *don't want* to argue with you, but I can't stop myself from doing it. I hate myself for it. I hate being like that, picking fights, making a big deal out of nothing … but I *can't stop*. I hate being like that, but I can't seem to help myself.'

'It's not that bad …' Siddhant said. 'I mean sometimes it's my fault too … I say and do dumb things all the time.'

'You are pretty dumb, yes.'

'Yep.'

They both nodded seriously, then burst out laughing.

After a moment, Akriti said, 'But seriously though, you've been so good to me. The best. I feel like an asshole for giving you such a hard time.'

'Stop it! It's hardly that bad.' Siddhant couldn't deny that it felt good to have some of the blame shifted away from him, but given the circumstances, Akriti was allowed to be a little irrational at times.

'Still, I feel bad. And you need to know that you've been the best boyfriend. You're all I have … And though I keep picking fights with you and hurting you and am an unappreciative asshole generally, I really do appreciate you.'

'I appreciate you saying that, but seriously, you have to stop now,' Siddhant said. 'After everything you've been through, you deserve to be a little unreasonable at times. And if you sometimes need a punch bag to let out your pain and frustration – I'm happy to be that.'

'No!' Akriti protested. 'Don't ever say that! It's not fair to you. And I don't want you use you as a punching bag. I love you. And I want to love you and care for you.'

'Not punch me?'

'Never!'

Siddhant laughed. 'That's good to know.'

Akriti leaned forward and hugged him. They stayed like that for a quiet moment, before she said, 'Sid, I love you.'

'I love you too,' Siddhant said. He kissed her cheek before getting to his feet and pulling her up with him. He sat her down on the couch and took out his phone. 'How does pizza and a movie sound? In my experience, I've found that a full stomach and some distraction can be very helpful in providing comfort. Which we both need.'

'That sounds good,' Akriti said, smiling.

'Great – suddenly our biggest problem at the moment is what toppings to get,' Siddhant said light-heartedly.

'Pizza solves everything.'

'Agreed.'

An hour later, they were lying together on the couch, Siddhant's arm wrapped around Akriti, who was resting with her head on his chest. A couple of slices of leftover pizza sat in the box on the table in front of them, while a movie played on the television. It was the most relaxed they'd been in many many weeks.

'I would like to stay the night,' Siddhant said casually.

'Really?' Akriti raised her head and looked at him. 'That's a little forward.'

'I have no shame.'

'Clearly.'

'So?' Siddhant prodded.

'Yeah, okay.'

'I can stay?'

'You can stay.'

'Win,' Siddhant muttered under his breath, just loud enough for Akriti to hear it.

Akriti smiled and rested her head back on his chest.

'Hey, not to spoil the mood or anything,' Siddhant said warily, 'but there's something I need to say to you.'

He felt Akriti stiffen. She pulled away to look at him. 'Yes?'

He hesitated for a moment. 'Do you think you should get some professional help? Talk to someone?'

'Are you saying I'm crazy?'

Siddhant froze. Had he overstepped?

But then Akriti relaxed. 'I'm kidding, Sid. We're doctors; of course I know how important mental health is.'

Siddhant relaxed too. 'I think if you have someone good to talk to, who has experience helping people navigate personal loss, you might really benefit from it.'

Akriti nodded thoughtfully.

'In any case, there's nothing to lose, right?' Siddhant watched her expression closely. He was really concerned about her well-being and wanted to help her, but he could only do that if she took the situation seriously too.

'I'll think about it,' Akriti promised.

'Good.'

He kissed her forehead, making her smile. Akriti leaned in and rested her head on his shoulder, facing the television.

'One last thing,' Siddhant said. 'When you're having a hard time, please tell me? I don't want you to go through it alone. When you miss your dad, and you're sad, just try to include me. If I don't know how you're feeling, I can't hope to help you, and it kills me. Don't shut me out, please.'

In response, Akriti burrowed her face in his shoulder and kissed it.

Chapter 10

'What's keeping him?' Siddhant said to no one in particular.

'I don't know,' Akriti said, looking down at her phone.

They were at the hospital cafeteria, but Prachi was the only one eating. Siddhant's shift had ended an hour ago and Akriti's was about to begin. She was keeping Siddhant company while he waited for Priyesh to finish surgery. Siddhant and Priyesh were going to see the new Guardians of the Galaxy movie with some of their friends from the hospital and Siddhant was worried that if they took any longer, he might fall asleep right there on the cafeteria table.

'What time's the movie?' Prachi asked through a mouthful of food. She chewed animatedly, gulped it down and spoke again, 'Sorry. I can't operate on an empty stomach. Not with my history of fainting.'

Siddhant laughed. 'It's in thirty minutes. But the first thirty minutes are just trailers, so we technically have an hour.'

'True dat.' Prachi's mouth was full again.

Akriti looked up from her phone. 'Babe, I've gotta go. Meghna just texted. There's a big emergency neuro case. I *have* to grab it.'

'Go!' Siddhant said excitedly. As he watched her gather her stuff in a rush, a part of him wanted to go with her. Complicated surgeries were swiftly becoming his most favourite thing. As he watched Akriti wistfully, his phone buzzed on the table, distracting him.

When Siddhant looked down at his phone, he did a double take. Maybe he'd read the name wrong. Nope, it really was Maahi's name, next to the little speech bubble icon. Why was she texting him? As he picked up his phone to look, his mind went completely blank. The world around him fell silent in that moment and the only sound he could hear was a thumping in his ears.

For reasons Siddhant couldn't explain, this felt surreal. The short buzz of his phone on the table, her text popping up on his screen – it took him back to when they were together, and had texted each other throughout the day. It was nothing out of the ordinary; it was something they did without thinking, a habit.

But not anymore. He read her text quickly, without fully taking it in. Something about her bakery and a coffee shop … He tried again, slowly this time. But before he could absorb the message fully, a soft touch on his arm jerked him back to present.

'What?' he said hastily.

'I said I'll see you at home,' Akriti repeated.

'Yes, yes, see you. Good luck with that surgery.'

Akriti waved and left. He was left alone with Prachi, who was still stuffing her mouth with food, and the message from Maahi. He read it again:

Hey Siddhant! Nice (and awkward) seeing you the other day. Something cool happened today – we're doing a collab with Roast House. Our stuff's going to be sold in 168 stores across India! We're SO EXCITED. Had to share! – Maahi

Before he could think about it more, he felt a tap on his shoulder.

'Yo!' Priyesh said. He was accompanied by Deepanshu, another resident at the hospital. 'How goes it?'

'Hey,' Siddhant said, getting up. 'You guys ready to go?'

'Yep, let's do it,' Deepanshu said.

They said bye to Prachi, who was finally close to wrapping up her meal, and headed out of the cafeteria.

'Should we take my car?' Siddhant asked.

'Works for me,' Deepanshu said.

'I'll come with you too,' Priyesh said. 'But you'll have to drive me to work tomorrow.' When Siddhant nodded, he continued, 'The movie's supposed to be really good. I heard Chris Pratt really kills in it.'

'Did you know that Batista plays Drax the Destroyer?' Deepanshu chipped in.

'Oh yeah, think his real name is David Bautista or something. Or Dave …'

Siddhant found his attention wandering as he walked to the car with his friends. Should he respond to Maahi? What should he say?

As far as he could tell, it was a casual text, with no deeper meaning or purpose, but he couldn't decide how to respond.

He was happy for her, about this collaboration. He had seen her build her company from scratch, and work very hard to make it successful, so he wanted to congratulate her on that. But he suspected this was one of those times when the content of the message itself was less important than the actual act of messaging. Given their history, this was less about what she had said, and more about the fact that she had texted him. For a moment, he wondered if he was overthinking it. For all he knew it was just an innocuous text about her work that she probably wanted to share with him because of their conversation a few weeks ago. But then she was his ex-girlfriend, and they hadn't texted each other since their break-up, so it wasn't that simple.

He had never been the kind of person to keep in touch with exes or have a friendly relationship with them post separation. However, he hadn't had a proper relationship until Maahi. If he didn't count high-school crushes and inconsequential dates, she was his only real ex. He didn't think there was anything wrong in texting her back, because they hadn't ended things on bad terms them; it probably wouldn't mean anything. But he remembered all too well how Akriti had responded to them randomly bumping into Maahi. He tried to imagine how she would feel or what she would say if she found out that he had texted his ex. There was no scenario he could imagine where this would end favourably for him.

Unable to make a decision, Siddhant hoped the movie would take his mind off his current predicament, which would also allow him time to figure out how to respond to Maahi. And once the movie started, he did find himself caught up in the action, but Star-Lord could hold his attention for only so long. Half an hour into the movie, he pulled out his phone, turned the screen brightness all the way down, and sent Maahi a text. It didn't take long, because he'd already gone over the words in his head a dozen times.

> Hey Maahi, Nice (and awkward) seeing you the other day too. Congratulations on the collaboration with Roast House. Sounds like an incredible new opportunity for you guys. – Siddhant

Having sent the text, Siddhant leaned back in his reclining chair. There. Done. Now he could focus on the movie. However, during intermission, while they waited in line to get popcorn, Siddhant found another text from Maahi waiting for him on his phone.

> I know who you are! You don't have to sign your name at the bottom!

He couldn't help the grin that appeared on his face as he read the message. He'd thought it was funny and weird that Maahi had said '– Maahi' at the end of her text, and had therefore given her a taste of her own medicine. He texted her back before returning to his seat, still smiling to himself.

> Right back at you :)

The rest of the evening was uneventful, apart from the events taking place on the big screen. He hadn't seen the first Guardians of the Galaxy movie, but even without having seen the first one, he found Vol. 2 to be very entertaining. He partook in the burning topics discussed by Priyesh and Deepanshu, who were both big devotees of the Marvel universe.

Before driving home with Priyesh, Siddhant checked up on Akriti, who was having a slow night at the hospital. He thought of his bed the entire ride home, eager at the prospect of sleep. A funny feeling was warming his chest, something he couldn't put his finger on, but he felt ... gleeful. Nothing outwardly dramatic, just a quiet happiness within.

Or it could be the absence of sadness. A lack of gloominess, that lifted his spirits. He caught himself checking his phone a couple of times, and then putting it away, a little disappointed, a little guilty.

Back in his bedroom, he pulled an old T-shirt over his head, his eyes glued to the screen of his phone, which lay face-up on his bed. He was pulling on a pair of sweatpants when the screen lit up. His heart raced, and he hopped to the bed on one leg. Not bothering to finish wearing his pants, he grabbed his phone and swiped it open. There was a message from Maahi.

Touché.

His heart beat loudly in his chest, as responses flooded his mind. He tried to pick a way to respond to her one-word text in a way that would keep the conversation going. If he responded with an emoji, it would essentially put a fullstop at this point in the conversation. If he said too much, he'd come across as too eager. Maybe he … He caught himself. This wasn't a game.

This was Maahi. The easiest person in the world to talk to. In all the time he'd known her, it was one of the things he admired about her the most. Even when she herself was confused, she was always straightforward and expressed herself honestly. If he wanted to ask her about the collaboration, he could just ask her.

But before he framed his message, his screen lit up again.

And thank you! We really are thrilled + terrified!

Siddhant responded instinctively.

Terrified? In a good way, I hope?

Haha, mostly. It's just that there's a lot
at stake now that we've actually won it. We
thought winning was the hard part,
but now we have to deliver …

Oh, come on. You know you've got
this. Clearly, they think so too

It took persuasion. It was almost like some
reality TV crap. We had to compete against
dozens of other bakeries and there were several
rounds and all that. Crazy!

Wow, sounds like a big deal *clapping hands*

I'd say so *upside down smiling face*

> So, what's the next step? How soon
> can I get your cupcakes at a Roast
> House near me?

It's going to take a while. We need to scale
WAY up. Not to mention, our products are
perishable, which complicates things

> I'm sure they have a structure in place
> to support the scale up. Roast House is huge

Truth. We only really need to focus on the
production part. They've got transport,
storage and distribution down

> And marketing, I'm sure

That too. Probably one of the biggest plus points

> No kidding. You guys are going to
> blow up *grinning face*

Yep *nerdy face*

Siddhant set his phone down for a second, and finished
putting his sweatpants on. He wanted to talk to her more. It

felt so good to talk about positive things. This was allowed, he reasoned with himself. There was no reason to feel guilty; it wasn't like they were flirting or anything. They were simply having a conversation. Old friends catching up. End of story.

Still, his mind wandered to *What will Akriti think?* But then he convinced himself that it would be fine. Akriti and he were in a better place and he had nothing to hide. If someone was to read through these messages, they would see that it was just a friendly conversation between two people. So then why couldn't he explain the lightness in his heart? He typed another message before he could stop himself.

So, how is everything else? How is your family doing?

Moments later his phone buzzed.

Things are good. Maa and Papa are
proud of me for a change, and not gonna
lie, it feels great *smiling face with sunglasses*

I bet! And what's Sarthak up to now?

He's in Mumbai – almost an aeronautical
engineer now, if you can believe it!

Good for him. Does he enjoy it?

Oh yes, it's all he talks about. He's having
the time of his life at that college

Well, at least someone in your family enjoyed
college *face with stuck-out tongue*

Yeah, yeah. Make fun of me.
I did okay for myself *smirking face*

Clearly! I was jk

I know! But enough about me. How are you?

I'm okay. Can't complain

That doesn't sound super positive ...

Nah, I'm fine

Are you sure?

Yeah. Work's good. I'm really enjoying it now

That's good. Cuz, you know, if you hate
your job, people will literally die ...

Haha, I'm aware. Thankfully, I love
my job. It helps that I'm getting good at it

Oh isn't that the best? Doing something
you KNOW you're good at?

The best *face with starry eyes*

I'm so happy for you! How's Priyesh, and
your other friend …? I can't remember her
name. The one that was lying face-down
passed-out on your couch when I came over
to your place for the first time, remember?

Hahaha, how can I forget? The day the
three of us played Mario Kart and
we kicked your butt

I had never played before!

Excuses. And they're both good. Priyesh
and I still live together, actually

First of all, I can beat you now. I have
gained experience playing with Laila and
her boo JD. And good to hear about
Priyesh, I always liked him

First of all, that's not possible. And
Priyesh liked you too … especially beating
you at Mario Kart

Jerk!

Haha, I'm only stating the truth

Yeah, the truth is too much in my
half-asleep state. God, it's after 1

 Weird thing, time. Okay, I'll let you go now

Okay, well, it was (mostly) nice talking to you

 Yeah, (mostly) good catching up with you too

Ugh you're so annoying

 That's me *grinning face with smiling eyes*

face with rolling eyes

 Okay, I'll stop

Thank you *slightly smiling face*

 Good night

Bye! *smiling face*

Shortly after the message exchanges, Siddhant fell asleep.
Yet, deep and far into his slumber, the conversation stayed,
never leaving his head.

Chapter 11

Akriti was not pleased.

Siddhant kept telling himself that it wasn't him, and he shouldn't take her moods personally, but at times, when her displeasure was directed solely towards him, it was hard for him to remove himself from the equation. They were at his place, and he was trying to convince her to go to a comedy show he was excited about seeing.

'Are you sure?' he asked, softly, cajoling.

Akriti rolled her eyes, and took a deep breath. Then she spoke deliberately, as if talking to a child who wasn't very bright, 'How many times do I have to say it?'

Siddhant paused. It hurt him when she treated him like that, but he kept reminding himself that she didn't mean it. 'I know you've told me you don't want to go. But I got tickets over a month ago. Remember, you said you really like these guys and wanted to see them live—?'

'Well, I changed my mind!' Akriti snapped.

'Akriti,' Siddhant said slowly. 'It's okay if you don't want to do this. We can do something else. Maybe stay here and—'

'You don't have to stay; I'm not stopping you.'

'I don't mind! I'd much rather spend time with you—'

'Oh, please! Spare me.'

'I'm serious,' Siddhant said patiently. Sometimes her irritability with others turned into insecurity and self-doubt. Siddhant had taken upon himself the task of pushing those thoughts firmly away from her mind when that happened. He didn't always succeed, but he never quit trying. 'I really would much rather stay here with you than go to that comedy show alone.'

'You don't have to go alone. Take Priyesh.'

'I'll give him the tickets, he can take someone else. I'll stay here with you. It's settled—'

'Oh my God! Can you stop being so … so …' Akriti looked around, her face crumpled in frustration ' … *nice* all the time.'

'What's wrong with me being nice to you?'

'You're smothering me! I don't need you to stay back and watch over me, I don't need your pity. Just go.' Akriti said firmly.

Siddhant was familiar with that tone. It meant that there was going to be no further discussion on the topic. He was used to this treatment now; he even expected it. Because her mood swings had been particularly violent in the last month, he had looked for help on the internet. He read several articles about how to support a loved one who was dealing with a loss, because her symptoms indicated that she was depressed. He was going by the book on this one. He made sure to tell her frequently that he was there for her, and that he cared about her. But he had to be careful not to say it too often and run the risk of annoying her, which seemed to happen increasingly of late.

On her low days, he would propose ideas of activities that would take them outside. But he would do so carefully; if she seemed resistant, he didn't push it. He gave her the freedom to make her own choices. And in her own time.

Sure, there were times when she snapped at him, or was rude to him, but he understood that she didn't mean it. How she behaved was a result of how she felt, and she couldn't help how she felt. For the first few months, Siddhant had assumed that her emotional turmoil was rooted in a deep sense of loss. He himself couldn't even imagine losing a parent, and was not sure how to help her overcome this profound loss.

It wasn't until he saw her leave their group of friends one day, a perfectly good day on which nothing went wrong, and slip away to the backyard to sit alone, doing nothing, that he realized she may be depressed. She was losing interest in pretty much everything happening around them. She wasn't excited about cases at the hospital anymore, was withdrawing from social interactions, wasn't sleeping or eating well, and was always in a bad mood.

None of these signs, Siddhant realized, were new. She had gradually been slipping into depression ever since her father had passed away. He remembered her sudden outbursts, followed by elaborate appeals for forgiveness. The way she would shut people out, including him, and later vent her anger and frustration out on him. Her intense mood swings. The time she was upset with him because he hadn't said 'I love you' back – when she had gone off the grid, skipped work, turned off her phone, leaving him to look for her everywhere until he finally found her at her apartment. And after he'd said 'I love you' to her the first time, how she had made it a habit to say it to him numerous times a day for several weeks, and then stopped abruptly. The day she got angry when he had complained about his parents and how guilty she had made him feel for criticizing them, when she didn't have any. Or the day she had planned the special surprise for him at his place, and the night was ruined just because he had made a simple comment.

On the other side of all of these episodes there had been a white rose and a heartfelt apology.

From his training as a doctor, and his research on the internet, he had concluded that she was exhibiting symptoms of depression. In the throes of emotion, she forgot where to draw the line, exhibiting anger and irritability the most. More often than not, those symptoms were directed towards him.

He was okay with it. As a doctor, he understood that like any other illness, the symptoms weren't her fault. But on an emotional level too, he cared about her, and wanted to be there for her and help her. If the only help he could provide was by being a punching bag, he would gladly be one.

There was something to be said for being there for her, and creating a supportive environment for her, but over time he had been feeling more and more inadequate. Even after all his research, and everything he had tried, he kept hitting a wall at every step. In the past month, especially, she had completely shut him out.

'Have you thought about …' Siddhant began tentatively. He knew it was a sensitive issue with her, and wanted to broach it carefully. 'Talking to someone? A therapist?'

Akriti groaned. 'Sid, please.'

'Okay, okay.' Siddhant held up his palms in surrender. He added quietly, 'I just wanted to check, because I know you were thinking about it …'

'I am.' Akriti sighed, a lot calmer now. 'I have been thinking about it, I promise.'

'Okay, there's no rush. Take your time.'

'Thank you.'

'I just want you to feel better,' Siddhant said, bending to kiss her forehead.

Akriti gave him a smile, the kind that didn't reach her eyes, and refocussed her attention on her laptop. He hadn't seen a real smile on her face in weeks.

There were times when she included him in her thoughts, times when she shared with him, let him in. But this wasn't one of those. In times like this, when he was kept out, and therefore had no idea what was going on in her head, he had to be careful about not being too intrusive. He was trying his best to help her the best way he knew how, but he could tell that it wasn't enough anymore. Not for the lack of trying, but he was barely helping.

She needed help from a professional. They had talked about her going to a therapist on a few different occasions.

While being open to the idea, she was equally hesitant to take a step towards it. Siddhant didn't see any point in putting it off. Nevertheless, he had to respect her opinion, and give her the space and time she needed to make her decision.

Meanwhile, the worst they had to deal with were angry outbursts here and there, random episodes of sadness and despair, followed by moments of intense clarity and remorse – going around in circles. He had to make peace with the fact that his life and needs had been put on the back burner. Under the circumstances, her needs were priority.

Siddhant ended up going to the comedy show with Priyesh, after all. It was a Saturday evening, and Priyesh was eager to get out of the tentative plans he had made with his friends, because apparently, Priyesh's friends could never agree on what they wanted to do or where they wanted to go – which resulted in all sorts of arguments and wasted time.

'They act like we're still in school. Like we have all the time in the world,' Priyesh grumbled as they got in line to enter the auditorium. 'Some of us have jobs.'

'Come on, they're just … more relaxed with their time. Most people loosen up on weekends, you know?' Siddhant smirked.

'Shut up! I can loosen up fine. I just don't want to chaperone a bunch of kids blowing their dads' money. At hookah bars, no less. Seriously, they need to grow the fuck up.'

'Whoa. You okay, dude?'

'Yeah. Yeah. It's just sometimes … it gets to me. We work so hard, and want to protect our free time. I don't want to spend it trying to get a group of grown up children to come to an agreement about how to spend an evening. It would be midnight before we even left the house.'

'Good thing you don't have to do that tonight,' Siddhant said. He looked up at the poster of the show and added, 'You sound like someone in need of comedy.'

'You bet. Are these people supposed to be good?'

'I think they're brilliant. I've been to their stand-up shows before, but this is a completely new set they're going to perform tonight. Been hearing great things about it.'

'Sounds promising,' Priyesh said.

Once inside the auditorium, they found their seats and settled down in the dark. The ninety-minute set didn't feel too long. Time seemed to fly as the auditorium became a laugh machine. Siddhant couldn't remember the last time he had laughed this hard. By the end of it, Priyesh's foul mood had disappeared completely.

Siddhant wished Akriti had come; she could use a laugh. The set had mostly revolved around politics and current affairs – essentially a satire on the government. He wondered, however, if it would've been her cup of tea. Despite having been with her for almost half a year, he sometimes felt as though he didn't know her at all. They'd skipped the getting-to-know-each-other part of the relationship, and jumped right into a boyfriend–girlfriend situation. He spent his time and energy trying to be her boyfriend, but the reality was that sometimes, his girlfriend felt like a stranger to him.

The thought gave him pause. It was the first time he had thought about their relationship like that. And now that he had, it made perfect sense. They'd never got a chance to get to know each other in the beginning, and in the time that they'd been together, the focus had been on keeping her happy; they hadn't got around to learning each other's interests. Sure, he knew about her family, her moods and quirks, her friends, her everyday life, but there was a big gap when it came to his knowledge of her likes and dislikes.

Half the time, she wasn't in a mood to talk. And when she did, every topic ended up leading to her father, her family, her loss. She never took an interest in his life, his friends, never even asked him how his day had been. Everything was always about her.

Siddhant felt guilty as soon as this thought crossed his mind. He wished he could take it back. She had been through something terrible, she deserved to make it all about her. He was wrong to feel this way when her pain was so much bigger than his little problems. It was just that sometimes he felt as though he was losing his identity trying to care for her ...

'You were right. They are very good,' Priyesh said, interrupting Siddhant's chain of thought.

'I told you,' Siddhant responded absently. Before he had a chance to completely shake his thoughts about Akriti away, he heard someone call his name as they exited the auditorium. Both Siddhant and Priyesh looked around to see who it was.

'Laila?' Siddhant squinted in the semi-darkness. There was a group of people, but he could distinctly make out Laila's profile in the centre, with Maahi on her side.

'I told you it was him,' Laila said to Maahi before turning to Siddhant. 'Hey man, how's it going?'

'Good. How have you been?' Siddhant said.

'Good, good,' Laila said. 'Just out here, trying to get a dose of laughter. By the way, this is JD, my boyfriend. And that's Ekta, Utkarsh and Gagan. And you know Maahi.'

'I know Maahi too,' Priyesh chipped in, looking at Maahi. 'Do you remember me?'

'Of course!' Maahi said, stepping forward to hug Priyesh. 'How are you? So good to see you!'

'Really good to see you too!' Priyesh grinned. 'Wow, I'd forgotten how pretty you are. Or do you just get hotter every day?'

'Are you hitting on me?' Maahi cocked her head to the side.

'What if I am?'

'It's not working.'

'Are you sure?' Priyesh raised his eyebrow. He probably thought he was being charming, but he came across as ridiculous to Siddhant.

'Pretty sure,' Maahi nodded fervently, laughing.

'Can't blame me for trying …' Priyesh grumbled.

Still laughing, Maahi turned to Siddhant. 'I forgot you were a fan of this group! Wasn't tonight's show the best?'

Before he could respond, Laila chimed in with, 'Maahi wanted to see this show so badly. Dragged us all here. Made us buy tickets like months ago.'

'They sold out within the hour! We *had to* buy them as soon as sales opened. And you can't say you didn't like it. You were laughing the whole time.'

'That I can't deny,' Laila said.

'It was a very good show,' Siddhant said. 'Definitely one of their best sets so far.'

'Right? I thought the Pappu jokes would get old quickly, but nope. Still hilarious,' Maahi said. 'The bit where they compared Modi to—'

'We're blocking the exit,' Laila interrupted, ushering them out. 'So Siddhant, do you guys have plans tonight?'

'Priyesh might hang out with his friends after we leave here,' Siddhant said, looking questioningly at Priyesh as they walked out.

'Nah, I can't deal with them tonight,' Priyesh said.

'So, no then,' Siddhant said to Laila. 'No plans for the rest of the night.'

'Why don't you come with us? We're celebrating Maahi's birthday tonight. Next stop – a rooftop in HKV that I think is outdated, but the birthday girl is partial to, so …'

'Oh, happy birthday,' Siddhant said to Maahi. He knew that it wasn't her birthday that day, but he kept that to himself.

'Thank you. It's not until next week, but we decided to celebrate early, because we're going to be travelling for work on the day of,' Maahi explained.

'So, what do you say?' Laila asked.

'I'm down,' Priyesh said.

Siddhant looked from Priyesh to Laila to Maahi. The night was still young, the weather was perfect for a couple of drinks on a rooftop … but he was worried about Akriti. However, she had made it clear that she didn't want to go out that night … and he wanted to go. Besides, it would be rude to say no to Laila.

He nodded in agreement, making a mental note to call Akriti from the car.

Chapter 12

Siddhant slipped his phone back in his pocket. He'd called Akriti twice from the car, but she hadn't answered. He figured she had fallen asleep. It was only a little after ten, but she'd had a migraine all day, so it wasn't unlikely that she'd gone to sleep earlier than usual. He left her a text message explaining where he was and decided to check on her a little bit later.

He returned to the corner of the rooftop where he'd been hanging out with Priyesh and either Utkarsh or Gagan. They were all holding bottles of beer that they'd pulled from the many buckets lying around. The party was much bigger than Laila had let on in her casual invitation – there were at least twenty people. A portion of the rooftop had been reserved for the party; there were four rustic wooden tables lined to one side, and the longest couch Siddhant had ever seen, spanning from one end to the other. Silver balloons with little cupcakes on them hung from the string lights above them.

Siddhant scanned the place and found Maahi within seconds. It wasn't hard, since his eyes had inadvertently been following her ever since they got there. Even though he pretended not to have noticed, he knew Maahi had changed her outfit for the party. She'd taken off the T-shirt she had on back at the comedy show, to reveal a shimmery violet top held together by very thin straps tied at her shoulders, tucked into her a sleek black skirt that ended a little below her knees, with a slit running up along one side. When she moved, her top caught light and came to life.

As if sensing his gaze on her, Maahi turned and looked right at him. When their eyes met, she gave him a big smile. Siddhant could only return a smile half as happy as hers. Her hair, which had been open at the comedy show, was now piled up on top of her head in a bun, several escaped strands floating around her face in the summer night breeze. But it was her lips that had Siddhant in a trance. As he looked at her, he remembered what it felt like to kiss those lips …

Siddhant caught himself. He quickly turned to Priyesh and focussed his attention on the conversation around him. Just because it felt like no time had passed and nothing had changed when he was around her, didn't actually change the reality. Things *had* changed. They *weren't* together. He couldn't afford to have these feelings. If their timing had been bad before, it was even worse now.

Shortly after, Laila got everyone's attention. A gigantic cake in the shape of a cupcake was brought out and set on the table in front of Maahi. The birthday song was sung, champagne bottles were popped, hugs were exchanged. Meanwhile, Siddhant fidgeted with his phone. He had tried calling Akriti again a few times, but she hadn't responded at all. He told himself that she must have fallen asleep, but a part of him wasn't convinced. The part that knew that nothing was ever really that simple with Akriti.

'Busy?'

Siddhant turned to look at the owner of the voice. Maahi was standing next to him, holding a glass of white wine, her beautiful eyes cheerful under the fairy lights.

'Hey,' Siddhant said, swinging the bar stool around to face her. 'Happy birthday. Great party!'

'Thank you! Mind if I join you?'

'Not at all.'

Maahi took the seat next to Siddhant. They were sitting by the ledge, facing the sky outside. They could hear the music coming from the bars around them, people chattering in the streets. 'Everything okay?' Maahi asked, gesturing to Siddhant's phone.

'Yes, just checking on Akriti.'

'Oh, is she okay?'

'Yes, yes. She had a migraine all day today, so I wanted to make sure,' Siddhant said. Because he felt strange talking about Akriti with Maahi, he changed the subject, 'Big turnout, huh?'

Maahi burst out laughing. 'Isn't it so dumb? Laila was adamant about making a big deal out of this, you know, because I've hit quarter century, so she invited everyone we know. Look at those buckets of drinks just strewn about all over the place. How ridiculous!'

'An onlooker may take you for a spoiled south-Delhi kid,' Siddhant said, smirking.

'Exactly. The horror! I'll let you in on a secret though – the owner of this place? He's friends with Laila's boyfriend JD, so he hooked us up. We're paying wholesale price for the liquor.'

'That sounds like a good deal. And happy twenty-fifth! All of this makes so much more sense now. You will be legally allowed to drink alcohol in the state of Delhi this time next week!' Siddhant laughed.

Maahi rolled her eyes. 'I've lived my whole life outside of the law ...'

'Yeah, you're the very definition of an outlaw.'

'Hey, don't make fun of me! It's my birthday party!' Maahi chided playfully.

Siddhant held up his palms in surrender. 'Sorry, sorry. You're right. It's your day. But imagine, in a week, you will no longer be cool. You'll be allowed to drink, no more rule-breaking required ...'

'I'm focussing on tonight,' Maahi said. She twisted her wrist to study her watch under the dim lights. 'Because for now, I still drink as an outlaw!'

'Cheers to that!' Siddhant smiled at her excitement.

They clinked their glasses, but Siddhant didn't take a sip out of his, which Maahi noticed. 'That's rude. You're supposed to actually take a sip after you say cheers ...' she teased.

Siddhant pointed to his phone, which he'd been holding in his hand the entire time he'd been at the party. 'I don't want to be rude, but I don't want to drink ...'

'In case you have to drive back?'

Siddhant nodded. 'Sorry for being a party pooper.'

'Oh stop. You clearly have bigger things to worry about,' Maahi said. She bit her lip and studied his face for a second before saying, 'I know you said everything is fine, but … are you sure? You don't seem to be doing so well. You don't have to tell me … You looked so stressed out just then, so I decided to butt in.'

Siddhant smiled at her, exhaling. 'The honest answer is – I don't know. Akriti has been dealing with some pretty big stuff these past few months, so we have our highs and lows. The only way I seem to be able to help is by being there for her, and so I try to check in with her every couple of hours …'

'I'm sorry to hear that,' Maahi said sincerely. 'When was the last time you spoke to her?'

'Before leaving for the comedy show. She hasn't been responding to my calls since …' Siddhant looked worriedly at his phone again, counting the hours since he'd heard from Akriti.

'Listen, I'm sure she's fine, okay? Don't worry. She's probably sleeping or something,' Maahi said. 'But I also think you should go check on her, just in case.'

Maahi spoke calmly, but Siddhant could sense her serious undertone. She was trying to reassure him. He couldn't remember the last time someone had come up to him and asked him if he was doing okay. His family didn't care; Akriti was self-involved (for valid reasons, he told himself, but self-involved nonetheless); and Priyesh had too much on his plate most of the time with hospital stuff, especially after the month-long bad streak he'd had.

He felt an unexpected tightness in his throat. Trying to avoid her eyes, he nodded at her as he rose. She stood at the same time, and his hand accidentally grazed hers as he turned to face the party.

'Sorry,' he muttered, feeling the warmth of her touch on his arm spread all over his body. Siddhant gulped and looked away. He was feeling ... emotions he wasn't ready to acknowledge. He snapped out it as Akriti's face flicked across his mind. He panicked. What if something was wrong? What if she wasn't okay? All thoughts of himself and everything else had left his mind. He had to go to Akriti. She might need him. 'I have to go.'

'Thank you for coming.'

Siddhant looked at Maahi's face, smiling up at him. They were now joined by Laila and two other people. 'Thank you for having me,' he said to Maahi, who rose up on tiptoe to give him a hug. 'It's going to be okay,' she whispered to him before pulling away.

Her voice, full of kindness and concern, rang in his ears as he walked away and searched for Priyesh. He located him, standing by a table with a group of people, and walked up to him. Once he was able to corner Priyesh, he said, 'I have to go back. Are you ready to go?'

'Now? Why? I thought we would stay longer,' Priyesh asked, looking around at the party. 'I like this place. Why do you have to leave?'

'I want to check on Akriti,' Siddhant said. He didn't offer any further explanation.

'Is something wrong with her? I mean, more than usual?' Priyesh snorted.

'Don't start,' Siddhant warned.

'Okay, okay. Sorry. I take it back,' Priyesh sobered up quickly. He set his beer can down and asked with sincerity, 'Is she okay?'

Siddhant felt a little stupid saying, 'I don't know. Maybe.'

'Why do you think she might not be?'

'I haven't been able to get in touch with her all night.'

'That could be nothing! Maybe she fell asleep?' Priyesh suggested. 'Or did something happen before we left? Did you guys get into another fight?'

'What do you mean by "another fight"?' Siddhant snapped, annoyed with the interrogation and Priyesh's perceptiveness.

'Just what it means, *another* fight.' There were no traces of humour in his tone. 'That's kinda what you guys do, right? Fight all the time?'

'Listen, I don't have time for this. I don't know what your problem with us is—'

'Not with you. Her. Why can't you see that she's fighting with you all the time, literally, all the time!'

'Priyesh, she suffered a big loss! Cut her some slack,' Siddhant said, louder than he'd intended. He lowered his voice and continued. 'I'm leaving. Are you coming or will you call a cab later?'

'You're going to drive? Haven't you been drinking?' Priyesh asked.

'Just water. I had half a beer when we first got here, but I'm good to drive now,' Siddhant said shortly.

'I'll come with you,' Priyesh said. He mumbled under his breath, 'Can't let you drive alone in this state ...'

'What state?'

'You're clearly … unhappy. You look like you've seen a ghost, and you're obviously worried about your girlfriend. I'm coming with you.'

'I'll show you a ghost …' Siddhant muttered as they made their way down the cramped staircase.

'Could you be more childish?' Priyesh shook his head at Siddhant.

'Just keep walking.'

❦

Half an hour later, they unlocked the front door and entered the apartment to find their living room dimly lit with the glow of the television. Akriti was sitting back on the couch, half her body cocooned in a throw blanket, her thumbs jumping up and down on her phone screen as she typed a text message. She glanced at them as they walked in and then turned back to the television, typing away on her phone as if she hadn't even seen them.

Priyesh threw Siddhant a pointed look and made his way to the fridge. He pulled out a water bottle and sat down on a bar stool by the kitchen counter. He clearly had no intention of leaving them alone.

Between his worry for Akriti, his freshly resurfaced feelings for Maahi and his annoyance with Priyesh, Siddhant didn't have a lot of energy to play nice or use tact. He walked over to Akriti and said simply, 'I called you.'

Akriti didn't turn around. 'Yes.'

'Multiple times.'

Akriti nodded.

'Why didn't you call me back? Or text me?'

Akriti shrugged.

'Was it something I did?' Siddhant was finding it hard to keep his temper in check. All this worry … for what? She'd just been sitting on the couch watching a movie and texting someone. She'd probably had her phone in her hand when he'd called her and sent her those messages. Why would she put him through hell for no reason? Who did that to someone they claimed to *love*?

Akriti got up from the couch deliberately. She met his eyes, and spoke in a low, cold voice. 'You leave me behind, to sit and wait for you, while you go have fun with your friends, and then you *happen* to run into your ex who's clearly still in love with you, and somehow end up celebrating her birthday? How convenient!'

Before Siddhant could process anything, she'd stormed into his bedroom and slammed the door behind her. Siddhant turned to Priyesh, his mouth open agape.

'I didn't plan to run into Maahi.'

'I know,' Priyesh said.

'She told me she didn't want to go to the comedy show.'

'I know.'

'Maahi isn't still in love with me …'

Priyesh shrugged.

Siddhant shook his head, in an attempt to clear it. 'How do I … What?'

Priyesh got up from his stool and levelled with Siddhant. For the first time that night, he didn't sound at all drunk. 'If you ask me … you're not allowed to be happy anymore. That has to be it. She can't stand your happiness and won't allow it.' He raised his hand to stall Siddhant's protests. 'I know what you'll say. I know she's suffered a big loss. But don't you see? You've lost yourself.'

Siddhant was stunned into silence.

'In everything you've done for her, she hasn't thanked you once. The walls aren't that thick, bro. I can hear her make your life hell – every single day. Ever stop to think about what you did to deserve this? She's just using you. She doesn't love you – she doesn't even know you! How long had you known each other before you decided you were partners for life? *Half a date!* Now you have a responsibility and she has a punching bag. I know you'll try to deny it, but it's true. You guys are playing house, pretending … but this is *not* what a loving relationship looks like. How can she be the love of your life when you don't even *know* each other! Open your eyes, Sid. She doesn't care about you. Period.'

Priyesh patted Siddhant on his shoulder before going to his room, leaving Siddhant standing there, thoughts swirling inside his head. He slumped on to a stool and rested his throbbing head on the counter. The cool granite felt welcome on his forehead. When his thoughts stopped churning, a face settled in his mind. Maahi. He was still in love with her. He would never stop loving her …

The thought came to him unexpectedly, but somehow, he wasn't surprised. It was a strange blend of being caught off guard and just knowing. He knew. He loved her, always had. His heart had never let her go. People were supposed to stop loving the other person when they broke up, but he simply hadn't done it. When they'd ended their relationship and gone their separate ways, he had left a part of him with her without realizing it, the part she'd claimed the very first day they met. She still had it. She'd kept that piece of him locked away, safe with her. And he'd carried her in his heart all along, while they had been broken up, hidden, untouched.

When he had stood next to her on the rooftop, surrounded by all those people, he had seen no one else. He'd felt this unrelenting urge to reach out and hold her hand.

I can't know her and not be hers.

As soon as the thought entered his mind, he knew it was true. But he *couldn't* be hers. So the only option he had left was to not know her. He couldn't talk to her anymore. The thought made his insides tighten in protest. Even though they weren't together, it seemed like they were breaking up – again. He remembered clearly how their break-up had felt the last time, and wondered where he would find the strength to endure that torture again.

He felt suffocated in his own skin. He wished he hadn't reconnected with Maahi at all. He would've been spared this glimpse of what his life might've been like with her in it. Then he could've been happy in his life … But would he really have been happy? If Priyesh was to be believed, he wasn't allowed to be happy anymore.

Siddhant lost track of time as he sat for hours on the bar stool, his head resting on the cool granite counter.

Chapter 13

Siddhant had the following day off, but he picked up a colleague's shift; he didn't want to stay home and think about his life. Akriti was still in his bedroom when he left, so he didn't go in. He had spent the night on the couch in the living room. He changed into a pair of scrubs at the hospital and spent the day shadowing a team of doctors. He didn't mind. Given how distracted he was, it was a relief not having to perform any surgeries. Being able to observe and learn kept his mind distracted.

By the end of the day, instead of feeling tired, he felt energized. He made his way home, his spirits dipping only slightly at the thought of facing whatever was waiting there for him.

The apartment was empty. Akriti was gone, but there was a white rose on the table. Taking it as a sign of peace, Siddhant was glad at the thought of their fight being over. However, a little part of him felt cheated by the lack of a real apology, which he believed he deserved. Akriti had accused him of being deceitful, of lying to her and going behind her back to have some sort of illicit liaison with his ex-girlfriend. 'Convenient,' she had called it.

He was hurt. All he had done from the second they'd met was be there for her and take care of her, put her needs and desires before his every time, and this was the treatment he was getting in return. Priyesh's words from the night before still rang in his ears … *She's just using you. She doesn't care about you.*

Siddhant shook away these thoughts. Priyesh didn't know Akriti or their relationship like he did. He didn't understand the dark place Akriti was in, and therefore couldn't comprehend her behaviour or actions. It wasn't her fault. She wasn't herself. When she did come back to her senses, she did sweet things like leave him a rose. Just because Priyesh hadn't seen her sweet side didn't mean it didn't exist.

Siddhant took the flower to his bedroom and laid it on top of the chest of drawers. He sat down at the foot of his bed and pulled out his phone. He had been thinking about Maahi, and how to move on from her; he had to say goodbye.

Hey, sorry for running out like that last night. Akriti is fine. Everything is good.

There. That was the last time he ever intended to talk to her. He couldn't bring himself to say anything else. This would have to be his goodbye to her – letting her know that he was with Akriti and everything was good.

He could take care of either Akriti or himself. And Akriti had no one else to turn to; he was the only one who would look out for her. Although it wasn't the most romantic or ideal situation, he understood his responsibility. He cared about her, so he would be there for her ... even though that meant no one would care about him.

A little later, he received a response from Maahi. He read it, set his phone down, and began trying to forget her, all over again.

Please don't worry about that! Glad to hear she's fine. :)

🌹

Siddhant buttoned down his shirt, checking his reflection in the mirror as he did so. He wasn't sure about the colour. It was a very dark green, which looked almost black, but not quite. It was as though it had tried to approach black but couldn't make it, and ended up being a muddy shade of green-black.

'Are you sure about this ...?' he asked Akriti, who was perched on his bed, watching him. 'The colour's a little off ...'

'Noooo, I love it!' she protested as she rose from the bed and approached him. 'I'm telling you, everyone's wearing this nowadays. It's a good colour. It's all about the deep moss right now.' She trailed her hand from his shoulder to his wrist, watching him in the mirror. 'Ah, I really do love it. Fits you perfectly.'

'If you say so ...'

'Come on! Don't be like that! Trust me, it's a great shirt.'

'Okay,' Siddhant relented half-heartedly. He could manage an evening in that shirt if it meant so much to her.

He tried to turn away from the mirror to find his shoes, but Akriti held him to his spot.

Snaking her arm through his, she inspected their reflection. 'We look so great together. Look, our outfits match perfectly.'

'That they do, but you look way better in that dress than I do in this shirt.'

'Aww, thanks, baby,' Akriti said, planting a kiss on his cheek. She released his arm and went closer to the mirror to inspect her lipstick. 'You're too sweet to me.'

Siddhant shrugged nonchalantly. 'It's what I do.'

Once they were dressed, they called out for Priyesh from the living room. One of the senior doctors at the hospital was retiring and they were all going to his farewell party. Priyesh yelled from his room that he'd leave later in his car.

'I don't want to stay out too late, okay?' Akriti said as they made their way out.

Siddhant nodded. 'You have that 9 a.m. shift, right?'

'Yep. Let's leave in an hour. An hour and a half tops. Basically just enough time for me to show off my dress, and then we can go home? Do you think people will think that's rude?'

'Doctors judging other doctors for caring about their careers? Nah! I'm sure they'll understand. We've all been there.'

'Okay, good. I don't know Dr Shetty anyway, and I'm still going to her farewell party. The charity stops there.'

Siddhant shook his head at her. Sometimes, when Akriti spoke like this about other people, as though she was better than them, he couldn't tell if she was serious. The first time it had happened it was about something ridiculous which they both laughed about. Then it became a thing, and began happening more frequently.

It had been a month since she'd left him the white rose after acting out about Maahi. Neither of them had spoken about it after that day. Siddhant had no intention of talking to Maahi again, so whatever suspicions Akriti did have about them, were unlikely to resurface. And even though Akriti hadn't actually apologized to him, her behaviour towards him had become much better. By an unspoken agreement, the incident wasn't discussed again.

When they arrived at the party, which was being hosted at Dr Shetty's house in central Delhi, they had to park a couple of houses away, because the roads were already lined with cars. At the door they were greeted by Dr Shetty's son and daughter. Siddhant gave the bottle of wine to the daughter and they were requested to go to the living room.

The living room was gigantic. The wall to his left was completely glass, overlooking a large pool in the lawn. Familiar and unfamiliar faces filled the living room and spilled on to the garden.

'Damn, I need a drink,' Akriti said, clutching his sleeve.

'Me too,' Siddhant replied, but his voice was lost in the bustle all around him. Holding Akriti's hand, he walked to the long table against the wall where two bartenders were serving drinks. 'I agree with you; we should leave early,' he said, handing her a drink.

'Right? Just being in this room is overwhelming,' Akriti agreed eagerly.

'I'll stick to a Coke then, so that I can drive us back.'

'What?'

Siddhant repeated his words, louder, in her ear. She nodded and gave him a thumbs-up. They spotted a group of doctors they knew from the hospital, and joined them. Soon afterwards, Prachi arrived and pulled Akriti out to the lawn with her.

An hour later, Siddhant was stuck in an even more crowded living room, pressed together with Priyesh and some colleagues. His back was sweaty and the noise was too much to handle. Worse, one of Dr Shetty's colleagues had cornered them and wouldn't stop talking. Every time this doctor, who looked not a day younger than eighty, spoke, he sprayed spit directly in Siddhant's face, who made sure to keep his mouth tightly sealed at all times.

'Yo, is your girlfriend okay?' an unknown voice yelled in his ear.

'Excuse me?'

'Dr Akriti Arora? Isn't she your girlfriend? She doesn't look okay. Been crying up a storm out in the lawn ...'

Siddhant caught Priyesh's eye before rushing outside. Priyesh followed him. They had to shout a little at the guests to make way for them. It was far more pleasant outside, but Siddhant was frantic as he looked around for Akriti. It only took a second. She was sitting by the pool, clutching her knees to her body, sobbing.

Siddhant ran to her, Priyesh at his heels. Prachi was crouching beside Akriti, holding her, and a few other people were gathered around them, watching.

'What is it? What happened?' Siddhant asked, panic-stricken. He was transported back to the night outside the restaurant, when Akriti had gotten the news about her father. His heart sank. 'Akriti, what's wrong?'

Prachi looked up at him, her face crumpled, a few tears smudged on her face. She didn't speak, simply stepped back and made space for him.

'Talk to me, Akriti,' Siddhant said, taking Prachi's spot.

Akriti sobbed harder.

'Please, tell me what's happened,' Siddhant was holding her tightly, his arms around her curled up body. He could feel her body shake as she tried to form words.

'I didn't even … I didn't know …' Akriti cried.

'What didn't you know?' Siddhant cajoled, speaking softly.

'He was only fifty-five … I thought he was healthy …' Akriti said, finally looking at him. 'And then ... he was just gone …' She couldn't continue, as her body was wracked with a fresh bout of crying.

The answer clicked in Siddhant's head and before he knew it, the words escaped. 'Your dad.' He was at a loss, and he doubted there was anything he could say to make her feel better. Nothing could bring her father back. All he could do was hold her.

So he held her as she cried.

'It's going to be okay …' he whispered to her. 'You won't always feel like this.'

'I don't know if I can do this …' she cried.

'You don't have to do anything.' He cradled her face in his hands and looked into her eyes. 'You've been so brave. The worst is over, trust me.'

Akriti's lower lip trembled and Siddhant pulled her back into a hug. He held her and murmured soothing words to her. Eventually, her cries softened.

'Akriti?' came Prachi's concerned voice from behind them.

Siddhant looked up at her, and then around. He'd completely forgotten about the rest of the world. He nodded at Prachi, and stood up. 'Let's go home,' he said and began to pull Akriti up. He righted her dress, which had ridden up by sitting on the floor. Glancing in annoyance at the people still surrounding them, who, instead of respecting their privacy and keeping their distance, were gawking at them, he muttered, 'People are watching …'

At once, Akriti jerked her arms out of his grasp and slumped down to the floor. She looked at him with venom in her eyes. 'I can't believe you,' she spat angrily.

'What …? What happened?' Even though completely thrown, he prepared himself for what was coming. As far as he could see, he hadn't done anything wrong, but then this wasn't the first time Akriti had had violent mood swings and flipped out on him. He saw another fight coming.

Chapter 14

'You're ashamed of me. I embarrass you.' Akriti spoke deliberately, rolling every word on her tongue before spitting it out.

'That's not true,' Siddhant said quietly, suddenly exhausted.

'You care more about what these strangers think than *my* feelings.'

'I don't. Akriti, please get up.'

'You just want to get me out of here because I'm *creating a scene*, isn't it? Isn't that what you want?'

Siddhant watched her, sitting stubbornly on the floor, with no intention of moving, simply because he had asked her to. He looked helplessly at Priyesh, who was standing there with his mouth hanging open, unable to believe the events unfolding in front of him.

'Akriti, please ...' Siddhant begged.

'Please *what*?' she retorted angrily. 'Say it. Say that I'm embarrassing you.'

Siddhant knelt next to her. He faced her squarely and said, 'No, it's not about that. I am *not* embarrassed by you. I am concerned about you. Two minutes ago, you were crying inconsolably in my arms. I'm just trying to take you home, because I didn't think you'd want to be here with so many people around us when you're feeling like this.'

She paused. For a moment, it seemed like she was listening to him rationally again. Siddhant latched on to the opportunity, and continued, 'Please, let me take you home. You'll feel better there, with some privacy. And we can talk about your fath—'

'Shut up!' Akriti thundered. *'How dare you?'* She got up with difficulty, stumbling because of her heels and her furious state.

Siddhant got up too, bracing himself to be accused for another thing he didn't do.

Akriti was shaking her head, utter disbelief etched across her face. 'How dare you drag my dad into this? I can't believe this …'

Siddhant's eyes didn't leave Akriti, but his ears burned, knowing everybody was watching, feeling their eyes on them.

A few months ago, Siddhant would've immediately been reduced to an apologizing mess, accepting all the accusations levelled against him. But this time, even if he discounted her behaviour because of her immense loss, he couldn't think of one reason why her outburst towards him was valid. She was publicly shaming him for trying to help her, and he was in no mood to simply stand there and take it. He couldn't allow her to treat him like that. Not anymore.

'That's enough,' he said. He spoke calmly, maintaining his composure. 'I'm leaving. You should come with me.'

'What the fuck does that mean?' Akriti snapped. 'You can't just *go*. I'm talking to you!'

'You're not talking to me. You're yelling at me. I'm leaving.'

Siddhant turned to Priyesh, who seemed to have returned to normal now, and they walked towards the house.

'Where are you going?' Akriti screamed after them, her voice breaking.

They kept walking. The crowd around them parted easily. No one at the party was focussing on anything else anymore. They were all watching Siddhant and Akriti.

'You can't just leave me here!!'

Siddhant halted, and looked over his shoulder at her. 'Then come with us. Come home.'

'No! I don't want to! You can't make me!'

Her voice was so loud, so frantic, that Siddhant could feel everyone around them get suspicious. By the way things looked, he wouldn't be surprised if they suspected that he was mistreating her.

Siddhant started to turn back to her, but Priyesh held his arm. 'We have to leave, dude,' Priyesh muttered. 'You're not doing yourself any favours by letting this go on longer. They probably think you beat her or something.'

'This is crazy ... You know I ...' Siddhant couldn't find words.

'Trust me, I know, but they don't. Let's just go.'

Siddhant didn't need further persuasion. He followed Priyesh out. Akriti was with Prachi and the rest of her friends. She would be fine. Just this once, he didn't have to be the only person responsible of taking care of her. And yet, as he walked through the restless crowd, he felt guilty for leaving her there.

How many times had he read about depression? How many times had he told himself that she was only lashing out on him because she was in a bad place and didn't know what to do? That she wasn't herself when she had episodes like this out of the blue? Yet now, when she was drunk and distressed, he was really going to give up on her and leave her there? Hadn't he promised himself that he would be there for her? So now when she was clearly in a crisis, he was just going to wash his hands off her and walk away?

He paused. 'Priyesh, stop,' he said.

'What's up?' Priyesh said, turning around. 'We have to go.'

'Not without her. I have to go get her. She's not okay. She needs—'

'Coward!' Screaming, Akriti caught up with them at the front steps of the house. She'd come around the house from the lawn, limping. She was clutching one of her sandals in her hand. Waving it in the air, she shouted, 'You're a coward. Such a *coward*.'

'Let's *go*!' Priyesh took Siddhant's arm and dragged him to the main gate. Several of the guests from inside the house had followed them out. 'If we stay here any longer, we're going to get beaten up by the mob.'

Siddhant didn't doubt that. He could hear snippets of conversation behind him, and sense the general anger of the guests – they thought he was abusive or that he had done something terrible to her. How had the night turned in this direction? Siddhant tried to understand the turn of events, but came up short.

He allowed himself to be dragged out of the main gate by Priyesh. No, he wasn't doing anything wrong by leaving her behind. She would be safe with her friends. He was not a coward for trying to protect his self-respect, regardless of what she shouted behind him as they left.

They sprinted towards their cars, but when Siddhant reached his, he realized that Akriti had the keys. She'd kept them in her purse before they entered the party. Turning around, he saw the same realization dawn on Akriti's face. She walked over to them, looking crazed, like she had no control over her own thoughts and actions, but was driven by some unknown force.

'Ha!' she laughed mockingly. 'That's what you get for trying to run away from me! You were just gonna leave me alone here, drunk, at a party? What kind of a boyfriend does that?'

'Sid, come with me. We'll take my car,' Priyesh said urgently.

Even though Siddhant knew there was no point trying to reason with her, he said, 'I didn't get you drunk. And you're not alone – all your friends are—'

'Right! How convenient. So that gives you the permission to just kick me to the curb?'

'Sid, just get in the car,' Priyesh insisted.

'But you've never been a real boyfriend, have you? Or even a real *boy* for that matter. Why can't you touch me?!

What are you hiding in those pants that you can't show me?'
Akriti said.

Siddhant was shocked. Her outbursts were nothing new
to him, but he had never imagined she would stoop to this
level of pettiness.

The honest answer to why they were not physically
involved with each other was that he was in love with
someone else. But even if Maahi hadn't existed, the
relationship between Siddhant and Akriti was more like
that of a nurse and his patient. There was nothing romantic
about it. Touching her felt wrong, as if he was taking
advantage of her when she was vulnerable. He could never
think about her romantically because he felt … imprisoned
by her.

'You call yourself a man?' Akriti challenged. Standing
there, holding his car keys in one hand and her sandal in
another, yellow under the street lights, slurring her words,
stumbling on uneven feet – she looked like she'd lost her
mind.

He couldn't leave her there.

'Siddhant, we have to leave *now*,' Priyesh begged.

'I have to get her,' Siddhant muttered, and walked back
to her. 'Just come with us, okay? We'll go home, and we'll
sort this out?' he pleaded with her. He reached for her hand,
because she looked like she was about to topple over, but
she slapped it away.

'Don't touch me!' she screamed frantically, as if he'd done
something terrible to her.

Siddhant backed off, raising his hands in surrender. This wasn't her. She wasn't in her senses. She needed help. He was failing. 'Tell me what to do, please,' he begged. 'What do you need? Tell me how I can help you.'

'I don't need your fucking pity. Who the fuck do you think you are?'

'Akriti, please, tell me what you need me to do—'

'Back the fuck off. I don't need you. I'm leaving!'

And with that, she marched to his car and let herself in. By the time Siddhant rushed to the door, she'd locked herself in. She started the car, and yelled, 'Get the fuck out of my way!'

'No! Akriti, this is insane!' Siddhant said, crouching by the window, panic settling like lead at the pit of his stomach. 'You can't drive like this! You're in no state to drive. Akriti, please …'

'Get out of my fucking way!' she screamed, her eyes flitting from one thing to another, as if she wasn't sure of what was happening around her. Her body was there, but her mind wasn't. Siddhant thumped on her window to try and snap her out of it, but it only made her madder. 'Just leave me alone!'

'Akriti! Akriti, please! Listen to me – we can work this out. We can talk about this. You'll be okay, just please get out of the car!' Siddhant said frantically.

'NO!'

'Please, Akriti, you can't drive like this. You'll hurt yourself! Please, listen to me …' But as he spoke, the car revved up, and he felt his heart drop. 'No, don't do this, Akriti, NO!'

She reversed, hit the car behind her, swerved, and in the next second, she'd sped off.

'Akriti, no! Come back,' Siddhant yelled after her, but it was too late.

'What the actual fuck!' Priyesh threw his hands in the air as he watched the car screech away.

'Let's go!' Siddhant said, frantic.

They ran to Priyesh's car, and wasted no time to follow her. It was a few minutes before they found her. It seemed like she was headed to their apartment, but her car was weaving and looked ready to crash.

'What the fuck is she doing?' Priyesh muttered, in the passenger seat.

'I think we should stay back. We should just follow her to make sure she gets home safe. If we try to stop her, she might ...' Siddhant couldn't finish the sentence. All of this felt surreal.

'Go crazy on your ass again? Yeah, I don't doubt it,' Priyesh said.

So they hung back, quietly following her. Siddhant grew anxious, watching her car zig-zag on the road. And then, she noticed them. That was the only explanation Siddhant could come up with for her wild honking on a relatively empty stretch of road. Immediately, he pulled over to the side.

'We can't follow her. She's not in control – she'll hurt herself if she gets more agitated,' Siddhant said, thinking quickly. 'We'll just wait here for a few minutes, and then head home. It's not far now, hopefully she'll get there safely.'

'Good thinking,' Priyesh said, clearly relieved that they had stopped.

'As safely as can be expected ...' Siddhant was shaking his head, his eyes wide and concerned, his mind racing to find a solution.

Probably in consideration of Siddhant's state, Priyesh kept his thoughts to himself. He wasn't a fan of Akriti, especially after the very public meltdown she'd just had, but in that moment he chose to remain silent, which Siddhant was thankful for.

And then, out of the blue, they saw her approaching them at full speed. She'd taken a U turn, and was driving on the wrong side of the road, heading right towards them, sounding her horn relentlessly.

Siddhant got only a few seconds to absorb what he was seeing. Even before he could reach for the key, Akriti crashed into their car with the ear-splitting crunch of metal on metal.

Siddhant's side of the door caved in, and he was thrown to his left, towards Priyesh. In the rush to follow Akriti, he hadn't fastened his seat belt.

The world became still.

'Oh god, oh god, oh god ...' Priyesh was muttering as he struggled to free himself from his seat belt. 'Siddhant! Are you okay? Siddhant ... talk to me, stay with me, no ...'

Siddhant's eyes snapped shut and the scene disappeared from before him. For a blissful moment, he didn't hear anything or feel anything ... then suddenly, his eyes shot open, and he felt every part of his body scream in pain. In the dim yellow light from the streetlight, he saw that their windshield had shattered into a million pieces. Siddhant's side of the car had crumbles, and pieces of metal had fallen out and were piercing his skin. Blood was gushing from a wound on his head, streaming down his face and seeping inside his shirt.

He tried to raise himself up, to see Akriti ... He could barely make her out in the darkness. She was pressed against the back of her seat, her head lolling to her side. Her body was completely still.

'No ...' he groaned, before slumping down, his head spinning, his lungs gasping for air.

'It's okay ... you're okay. I'm getting you out ...' Priyesh was chanting.

That was the last thing Siddhant heard before he lost consciousness.

Chapter 15

All he could tell for sure was that he was in a hospital. He was awake, but his eyelids refused to open. He tried to move his fingers, but his body couldn't make it happen. He tried to wiggle his toes, but with the same result. At long last, the most he could do was gulp. There was a terrible taste in his mouth. A sort of metallic taste that could be a mixture of blood and medication.

Siddhant stayed like that for a long time, awake but unable to move. He figured he was feeling the after-effects of a strong anaesthetic. Then, slowly, he began hearing voices around him, muffled at first, then clear … he understood some of the interaction. Doctors talking to someone … a woman whose voice he didn't recognize. And was that … Priyesh? *Priyesh*. Was he okay? He heard something about a miracle … but before he could hear anymore, he slipped back into an uncomfortable unconsciousness.

The next time Siddhant woke up, his mind was blissfully clear. He opened his eyes, blinking at the bright lights and took in the bland white ceiling with a fan hanging from it. Without moving his body, he looked around. He was in a shared room with another patient, an older man who seemed to be asleep at the moment.

He heard voices from the door, and strained his neck to see Priyesh standing there, blocking the way. Who was Priyesh trying to keep out? Siddhant tried to call out to him but all that escaped his mouth was a groan.

Priyesh spun around. He looked suspiciously at the old man first, before realizing that the sound had come from Siddhant. 'Hey man …' he said, rushing to his side. 'How are you feeling?'

'Medium,' Siddhant croaked. His throat was dry and it felt unusual to speak. 'You?'

'I'm okay. My left shoulder's got a bruise – I hit it against the door when … the crash happened.' Priyesh held his left arm by the elbow and threw a dirty look at the woman near the door before continuing, 'But that's all. I'm okay.'

Priyesh was nodding vigorously, as though unable to believe that he'd ended up coming out of the crash okay. Siddhant felt a pang of guilt, and said, 'I'm so sorry …'

'You didn't do it! I was there. You didn't do anything. It was that—' Priyesh caught himself before saying what he thought of Akriti.

'How's she?' Siddhant asked, his heart racing, the sinking feeling returning to his chest.

How had this happened? Why couldn't he have stopped it from going down like this? The image of Akriti's still form pressed up against the back of her seat, her head drooping on her shoulder, was still etched his in brain. It would always haunt him. What if Akriti …

'She's alive. They're saying she's in shock, but she's going to be okay. Your car has airbags, so she was protected,' Priyesh said, and then added after a moment's pause, 'I mean *had*. You don't have a car anymore. Neither do I.'

In the silence that followed, they both went over the scene from the crash in their minds. Siddhant wondered about how hurt he was. He almost didn't have the courage to ask Priyesh about his own condition. He was too scared to look down at himself, or move at all. His mind was clear, but his body felt as though it was still asleep. And to be a surgeon and do what he did, he needed both his body and his mind.

Before he could say anything, the woman loitering by the door finally walked inside. Now that Siddhant could see her clearly, he was able to place her immediately.

'Hello, Siddhant,' the woman said.

'You're Akriti's mom,' Siddhant said in response.

'Stepmom,' the woman said dryly. 'Don't let her hear you call me her mom. She's angry with you as it is.'

'She's angry …?' Siddhant blurted in disbelief, then kicked himself for even being surprised. This was not out of character for Akriti – to try to kill all of them, and then be angry with *him* for failing to do so. He'd stood by her through a lot of her crazy behaviour, but she'd crossed a line this time, by putting him and his best friend in danger, along with herself. This wasn't forgivable.

'She's angry that I was called. Your friend here is filing an FIR,' Akriti's stepmom said, motioning towards Priyesh.

'The police arrived at the scene and followed us to the hospital. Not that I was going to protect her by lying to them, but even if I were, those officers weren't stupid. We were in a *parked* car on the side of the road! She was drunk. *She tried to kill us!*' Priyesh's voice got louder as he spoke. 'The only reason she isn't locked up right now is because she needs medical attention. But believe me, there are officers outside her door. She isn't getting away with this.'

Before Siddhant could wrap his head around that, Akriti's mom spoke. 'Siddhant, please. You know she's not in her right mind. She needs help, she didn't do it on purpose—'

Priyesh cut her off angrily. 'She did do it on purpose! I was there. She *intended* to hit us head on. It was every bit intentional.'

'She would never do that! Not in her right mind!'

'Well then, she lost her mind, didn't she? She's been treating Siddhant like a slave for months and months, and the first time he stood up against her, she flipped her lid,' Priyesh fumed.

'Priyesh, please let me talk to Siddhant,' Akriti's stepmom said. 'I know what my daughter did to you both is unjustifiable and unforgivable. Trust me, I understand where you're coming from. But if you file an FIR against her, she will never get her life back. She will be tainted … her reputation will be ruined. She might go to prison! And with a criminal record like that, she might never be able to practise medicine again.'

'Good! She shouldn't be allowed to be a surgeon. What if her next breakdown happens in an ICU? She's a threat to herself and those around her,' Priyesh countered.

'I know it's a lot to ask, but please, please, consider this. I'm begging you, please don't destroy her life.' Her voice was pained. She seemed extremely tired, but her eyes were alert. 'I know it is a lot to ask, but please consider my request. I'm the only family she has, and she's the only family I have left … I have to look out for her. I can't let her go to prison …'

Siddhant was trying to process everything that had been said in the room. But before he could say anything, or even think clearly enough to form a thought, she spoke again.

'Don't decide now. Please, think about it,' she said, as she backed out of the room. 'I'll be with Akriti.'

There was barely a second of silence before Priyesh burst out, pointing at the door from which Akriti's stepmom had just exited, 'Is this woman crazy?!'

'Whoa! That's not nice,' Maahi's voice came from the door. 'Is that how you talk about me behind my back?'

'Not you!' Priyesh protested with a certain amount of frustration. 'Akriti's mom – she still won't give up trying to change our mind about filing an FIR,' Priyesh said. He turned to Siddhant and asked, 'We're filing an FIR, right? We *have* to!'

'Maahi?' Siddhant said, surprised at her sudden re-entry into his life.

'Hey,' she said, her brow furrowed in concern. 'How are you feeling now? You've been unconscious for two days; I ... we were all really worried.'

'Oh, right. I should go get his doctor,' Priyesh said, as if suddenly remembering that Siddhant was hurt. 'You hit your head against the steering wheel. The airbags didn't inflate. You were falling in and out of consciousness, so we were observing you for brain damage, potential concussion. I'll let them know that you're awake.'

After Priyesh left, Maahi turned to Siddhant. 'So? How do you feel?'

'Never better,' Siddhant said, half-grinning.

Maahi sighed, shaking her head. 'Your head's pretty banged up. Don't look at a mirror yet – your eyes are doing that whole swollen and purple thing we see on TV. And your right hand is pretty banged up – you have a hairline fracture. But you were all very lucky, overall. I saw the cars ...'

Siddhant absorbed that information, and then asked the first question that came to mind. 'Who called you?'

Maahi laughed. 'Funny story. Remember that time, when we were together, we talked about one of us being found dead in their apartment and the other person not knowing whom to call, and then we shared each other's families' phone numbers? And we also made each other our emergency contacts? Guess we never got around to changing that.'

'Ah.' Siddhant tried to nod but his head refused to obey.

'They called me the night of the accident. It was horrible.' As she said it, Siddhant could see in her eyes how distressing it must've been. They never could hide her feelings, those eyes. 'Priyesh was frantic. You were unconscious, with your face looking like that, your hand swollen. They wanted you to regain consciousness for some reason, so they kept trying to get you to wake up, but you … just lay there.' Maahi shook her head, as if trying to erase that moment from her memory. 'And Akriti kept screaming. She was unconscious too, actually, but then she woke up and I guess she must've been in a lot of pain, because I've never heard anyone scream like that. Her mom arrived shortly after, which only made the screaming worse. They had to give her something to make her sleep …'

'I'm sorry …' It was all Siddhant could say, 'Sorry that you had to see all that …'

'No! Are you kidding me? I'm just glad you … I mean everyone is okay. It really is a miracle. They were saying that because your car wasn't moving, Priyesh had his seat belt on, Akriti had airbags, and you saw what was coming and ducked … you're all okay. When I think about what could've happened …'

Siddhant stretched his hand to hold hers, and this time, thankfully, his body obeyed his brain's order. She squeezed his hand in return, and he knew that he would never stop loving her. In that moment, no matter how hard he tried to remind himself why they broke up, he couldn't think of a single reason good enough to keep them apart. If he'd died that night, he now knew, it would've robbed him of the chance to be with the love of his life …

Priyesh returned with a doctor and a nurse. They proceeded to give him a thorough examination and declared that he would recover in time, but would have to be kept under observation for a week. And that he couldn't return to work until the hairline fracture on his wrist had healed and he got a green light to operate again; Siddhant was looking at four to six weeks at least if there were no further complications.

It was only after the doctors left that Priyesh spoke up. 'I told you we needed to leave,' he said quietly. He was clearly holding on to a lot of anger and resentment, and not only towards Akriti and her mom.

'I couldn't leave her there—' Siddhant began, but he was cut off.

'Yes, you could've. You *should* have! She wouldn't have thought twice before doing that to you. Hell, she tried to kill you! And me – for no fucking reason. Don't you get it? Have you gone fucking blind?' The anger bubbling inside Priyesh boiled over.

Siddhant was too weak to speak, let alone argue.

'If you're not mad about the fact that she tried to kill you, by crashing your own car into mine, headfirst, for no reason, what about me? Are you at least angry that she tried to kill your best friend?'

'Yes, yes, of course—'

'Then tell me we're filing an FIR!'

Siddhant was silent.

'Put your money where your mouth is. If you care about me at all, tell me we're filing an FIR!' Priyesh insisted.

When Siddhant still remained quiet, Priyesh hit his breaking point.

'She deserves to get what's coming to her! She has to pay for her actions. It's attempted murder, don't you get it?'

Siddhant sighed, thoroughly drained. 'She's not a monster,' he said finally. 'That night, she wasn't in her right mind. You don't know her—'

'Neither do you!' Priyesh thundered, losing his composure. 'You knew her for half a date before you became her nurse, her punching bag, her driver, her lawyer … How many times do I have to tell you? Stop defending her, man, just stop! This is madness.'

'Priyesh, please try to understand …' Siddhant pleaded, 'Please, listen to me—'

'No! This is it. I'm out. If you want to ruin your life, go ahead. I'm done giving a shit. I'm leaving. I can't be involved in this nightmare anymore. I didn't put in a decade of studying and piling up student loans to come this far and have some crazy woman kill me. That is not my life plan. I'm moving out, and I hope I don't have to see you or that wretched woman ever again.'

'Priyesh …' Siddhant was in too much pain to stop him.

After Priyesh had stormed off, Maahi sat with Siddhant until he fell back into an uncomfortable sleep. He was jolted awake several times, by a nightmare or excruciating pain shooting through his body – but every time he resurfaced, he found Maahi's hand clutching his tightly. When he tried to speak, tell her what he'd seen in his nightmare, or where it hurt, she whispered into his ear, soothing him, calming him down till he fell asleep again. For the first time in a long, long time, Siddhant didn't feel absolutely alone in the world.

Chapter 16

In the week following the accident, Siddhant didn't see Akriti at all. He knew she had been brought to the same hospital, but since Priyesh hadn't visited him after he'd stormed out the other night, he had no news about anything that was happening in the world.

The day after Akriti's stepmom had first spoken to Siddhant about not filing an FIR, she came back to see if he'd given it any thought. When he told her that they weren't filing an FIR, she thanked him profusely and left. It was the last he saw of her.

It had been a lonely week for Siddhant. With no one to talk to, no work to distract him and only pain to keep him company, he'd barely had a good hour's sleep. He found himself going over events and arguments – with Akriti, Priyesh, Maahi – over and over again, tossing and turning all night, unable to calm down enough to fall asleep. His entire being was agitated.

Just because he hadn't filed an FIR, or agreed wholeheartedly with Priyesh's outlook on the situation didn't mean that he thought Akriti was innocent. He wasn't born yesterday. He knew Akriti, in whatever state she'd been in, had intended to hurt them. She had meant for the crash to happen, and she had intended for it to be much worse than it ended up being, thanks to her loss of control at the last moment, in her inebriated state.

He understood that his sense of responsibility towards her was misplaced. Perhaps it was rooted in the fact that he was with her when she got the news, or that he'd been able to help her in the beginning, which had made him feel useful – but then slowly, it had become his and only his job to look after her. His empathy, and the fact that he cared for her had put him in a situation where he had felt the need to make confessions of romantic love and want. Maybe he had hoped that he would mean those words one day soon. However, the moment he'd said them, she had labelled them 'boyfriend' and 'girlfriend' and expected them to behave as couples did with each other, despite their distinct personalities, temperaments and desires. They couldn't simply be themselves and be with each other, and let the connection grow organically into what it was meant to be. It was like being forced to sign up for a club and then being handed a set of mandatory rules and regulations.

Siddhant and Akriti had never had the freedom to find out who they were together. How they would interact with each other, discover each other …

There was a soft knock at his door. Siddhant looked up. 'Maahi,' he said, his pleasure obvious in his tone.

'You look *so much* better!' Maahi said excitedly, then calmed herself down before saying sheepishly, 'Erm … hi.'

'Hi.' Siddhant smiled. 'You don't have to look that excited; I'm sure I didn't look that ghastly when you last saw me.'

'Oh, you have no idea. If I hadn't been worried out of my mind, I would've collected photographic evidence of the ghastliness,' Maahi said, dead serious.

'Okay, that's enough,' Siddhant said, fake annoyed. 'Kicking a man when he's down. Real classy.'

'I just say it as it is.'

'Thank you for the blunt honesty then.'

Maahi finally relented. Laughing, she said, 'Too far? Sorry! But how are you, really? Has Priyesh been back at all since his dramatic exit the other day?'

'I feel okay. And no, I think Priyesh was serious. He really doesn't want anything to do with me anymore.'

'Oh no, that's not good. You know what, I'm sure he'll come around. Too bad he's a doctor and knows you're going to be okay, otherwise you could've played some emotional blackmail games on him,' Maahi said. Then, as if struck by a sudden thought, she added excitedly, 'Do you think he's been checking up on your status surreptitiously? Can he have access to your charts or reports or whatever? I bet he's been keeping an eye on them.'

'I wouldn't be so sure. He was really angry. I can't think of a time when I've seen him get like that. I think he's really done with me,' Siddhant said, not bothering to hide his sorrow.

'That's not true! He's done with … her. You know he cares about you. He's your best friend!'

Siddhant wanted to believe her. He couldn't not have Priyesh in his life. They'd known each other for over a decade and lived together for several years. He'd hate for something to create an irreversible rift between them. But for now, until he figured out things with Akriti, the best thing he could do for Priyesh was to keep his distance.

'Listen,' Maahi said, her tone serious. 'I've been thinking about something … Ever since that day with Priyesh, when he said all those things about how Akriti's been behaving towards you …' She paused, searching Siddhant's face for a reaction. When he didn't say anything, she continued, 'I know it's not my place … and I've kept my distance from you all week, even though it was really hard not to come visit you when you're hurt. But it's been bothering me, and I have to say something.'

'Okay,' Siddhant said. He'd never talked to Maahi about his relationship with Akriti, but if she believed what Priyesh had said, he could imagine what was coming. He braced himself.

'First of all, I know that I am probably way off base. I don't know Akriti or your relationship with her well enough to jump to any conclusions,' Maahi said. Siddhant could tell that she had rehearsed the words, and was gauging his reaction as she said them. 'But Siddhant, it's not okay to hit someone with a car! You don't see how insane it is, because you're in it – you understand the motivations and intentions behind her action. You make excuses for her because you know where she's coming from. But I'm sorry, I cannot be an innocent bystander. I refuse to let you suffer like this, and not do anything to help. I care about you too much to do that.'

She took a breath, before continuing, 'Siddhant, I have known you, I have loved you. And even though I made a stupid, stupid mistake that ended our relationship, it doesn't mean that I stopped caring about you.' She took his hand and looked him in the eyes. 'I have to ask … is she *mistreating* you? Let's forget about the car crash, let's say it was a one-off, a drunken accident. But apart from that one incident … in your life pre-crash … are you happy? Because I don't think you are. I could be wrong, but I have to ask.'

With his hand still in Maahi's, drawing strength from her warmth, Siddhant thought about that. The mere fact that someone cared deeply enough about him to sit down with him and ask him if he was happy made his throat tighten. He'd been bound to his hospital bed, alone, with no one to fuss over him. His own parents had only worried long enough to have the doctors send his reports to them and conclude that he'd be fine so they didn't need to fly down to sit by his hospital bed when they could be doing much more important work and advancing their careers. Priyesh had washed his hands off him, Akriti hadn't so much as texted him. Even Maahi … but she'd kept her distance because she cared too much not to say anything.

He was grateful that she had returned. And for that, he owed her honesty. He spoke gruffly, 'I haven't thought about my own happiness in a while. There've been bigger things happening, that I had to prioritize.'

'Is she abusive?' Maahi said abruptly, as if she'd been holding that one back for a while and it escaped her mouth before she could stop it.

'What? No,' Siddhant said. 'I know that she's crossed the line a few times, but she is dealing with something major which is impairing her judgement ... There's an explanation for her behaviour. She's not ... purposefully hurtful.'

'But she *is* hurtful. See, my problem is that while you've been putting your own happiness on the back burner, out of the goodness of your heart, she might've been abusing you,' Maahi said bluntly.

'She's not abusive—'

'This might be the first time the abuse manifested itself in physical form, but there are other kinds of abuse,' Maahi said firmly, before Siddhant could interrupt her. 'There's emotional abuse, sexual abuse, psychological abuse ... and I'm not saying that she's doing any of this on purpose, or that she's some kind of monster who's doing this out of spite—'

Siddhant shook his head. 'You've got it all wrong ...'

'Maybe I have, but give it a thought,' Maahi insisted. 'Do you feel free? To do what you want, within reason? Or do you feel like your freedom has been stolen? Because if you do, and you have to do or not do certain things because you're afraid of the repercussions ... it's not fair. And someone who loves you, and really cares about you would never let you feel like that, let alone do that to you. So, you don't have to tell me anything but just think about it. Because your happiness, your well-being are important too. Okay? Just think about it.'

Siddhant nodded slowly. She was clutching his hand tightly, desperately, as if she was in pain.

Maahi stayed with him for a long time, holding his hand in both of hers. Neither of them said anything more; they were lost in their own thoughts. Maahi removed her hand from his once or twice, to wipe the tears off her face, and when she returned it to its original position, Siddhant squeezed it in hopes of providing some reassurance. He felt touched, and overwhelmed. He knew what he had to do. He had known from the moment he'd seen Akriti drive towards them at full speed, horn blaring. Maybe he had even known when she had insulted him repeatedly in front of all their colleagues. Maybe he'd known from the beginning …

He couldn't be with Akriti. He had to end it. One would think that hitting someone with their car automatically implied a break-up, no discussion required, but he had to do it right this time. He had to end it with Akriti, once and for all.

❧

Later that day, when he was packing up his few things to be discharged and go home, he got a surprise visitor. Maahi had long left, and his mind was completely made up about Akriti. He felt some of that freedom that Maahi had spoken about coursing through his veins. He felt lighter, like he wasn't carrying as much weight on his shoulders anymore – until Akriti showed up at his door.

She didn't say anything, just stood there, her face bare, hair tied back in a bun, right leg in a cast, watching him. And then he noticed the white rose in her hand, and he felt the weight return to his shoulders, all at once.

Chapter 17

'Hi,' she said, watching Siddhant carefully. She kept her distance from him, lingering by the door instead of coming in.

'Hey,' Siddhant said. He found it hard to look at her, so he resumed packing his stuff. He had been so sure of what he would say to her, but now that she was there, he felt unprepared. He had to be firm and unwavering in his decision to end things, but he also had to be sensitive in the way he delivered the news.

'How are you?' Akriti asked. She took a couple of steps inside, and said, 'I'm really sorry, you know? About what happened that night.'

Siddhant paused. He couldn't help saying, 'About what happened? Or what you did intentionally? And no, I don't know that you're sorry. Never heard you say it.'

'I'm sorry,' Akriti said, her lips trembling as if on cue.

'Don't! Don't cry. We can't have a conversation if you start crying.'

'Okay ... okay.' Akriti sniffed, and tried to visibly compose herself. She held out the white rose in her hand, offering it to him. 'This is for you. For peace. I'm sorry.'

Siddhant looked down at the flower, his lips pursing. 'We could've died. All of us. Do you get that? What did Priyesh ever do to deserve that? What did *I*—'

'It's on me! All of it – I did it! It's no one else's fault, no one did anything to deserve it, I know that,' Akriti said in a rush.

This was enough to shut Siddhant up for a second; he'd never seen Akriti admit guilt like this, and take responsibility for her actions.

'I was so drunk,' she was saying. 'And so so sad. At that party, it hit me out of nowhere, and it … it felt like I was possessed. It took over every cell in my body. I literally fell to the floor crying, and I couldn't stop. It was the worst feeling ever, like I was being suffocated, like someone was pushing me down, down, down into the ground. And I couldn't get up. You don't understand … it was horrible.'

Her face was wet with tears, her eyes wide in horror. As if reliving that experience was too much for her, she hobbled over to Siddhant's bed and sat down. 'You can't even imagine, it was so painful. Like I had to dig through several feet of mud to crawl out of the earth I was being buried under. I just wanted to run away … And then I started lashing out, saying all of those terrible things to you. You think it was fun for me? Creating a scene, looking like a crazy person chasing you, screaming, in front of so many people? It was so embarrassing …'

Akriti looked up at the ceiling and closed her eyes, her body trembling. 'I couldn't breathe. I wanted to crawl out of my own skin … I felt so trapped, I just needed to escape somehow. There were moments when it felt as if I was watching myself, and I could see how insane I was. I *wanted* to stop – chasing you, screaming – but I couldn't. My own body was holding me against my will. You don't understand. I'd never felt like this before. I was completely helpless …'

'I was trying to help you,' Siddhant said quietly.

'Yes! And my brain knew that, but I couldn't stop myself from acting the way I was regardless. It was like I was *possessed*. I'm telling you, it was … scary. I couldn't control my own self. It was so so scary,' Akriti sobbed. She covered her face in her palms and shook her head frantically, as if to drive the memories away.

'I'm sorry you had to go through that. That sounds awful,' Siddhant said. He sat down next to her and placed his hand on her arm. 'Look at me, Akriti.'

Akriti removed her hands from her face and looked at him with red eyes.

'You need to get help. What you're describing … no one should have to go through that. There are people who can help you.' Siddhant spoke evenly. 'It is not okay to feel that way, and you don't have to. You can seek help, and get better …'

Akriti studied the floor, tears streaming down her face unchecked.

Siddhant paused briefly, trying to carefully pick his words. 'Akriti, after that night, you have to understand that we can't keep doing this. I can't be with you. It's not healthy. It's not good for either of us.'

Akriti's eyes shot to his, and widened in horror as if her worst fears were being realized. Siddhant softened his tone further. Saying the words that came out of his mouth next was one of the hardest things he'd had to do in his life. 'I don't want you hurt you, or place blame. I know how great your troubles are, the internal battles that you fight every day. I understand how crucial mental health is, and how adversely it can affect someone's life. I've tried so hard, for so long ... And I've been patient, you know that, but—'

'Don't do this, please, don't do this,' Akriti began muttering. 'Please don't do this ...'

'Akriti, I have no other choice. I have tried to be there for you, but I can't die trying to save you. I *can't* save you. I'm not what you need, I'm not well-equipped to help you—'

'I'll go to a therapist. Hell, I'll even go to a psychiatrist. Whatever you want,' Akriti said desperately. 'Just please don't do this ...'

'Please try to understand. We're not right for each other, we're not good together. We're not compatible—'

'I will work on it, I promise! I know I've been shitty to you, but please don't leave me. I'll do whatever you want. Anything! Just say the word and I'll do it, but just please don't leave me.' Siddhant tried to speak, but Akriti spoke over him, desperate to drown him in her words. 'You can't leave me. Not now! I can't do this by myself. You saw what happened the other night – I'm not okay! I need you! I can't do this without you. I can't live. I'll die!'

A stunned silence followed Akriti's words. Siddhant was afraid to look at her, and once he did, he couldn't look away. He saw something click in her eyes. All of a sudden, she didn't seem frantic or desperate anymore. She became calm; she knew what she had to do.

'I will die,' she repeated, deliberately. 'If you leave me, I won't be able to live anymore. You're the person closest to me. You know me best. And if you don't love me, no one does. I'll have no one. And I can't live with that. I will die.'

Siddhant felt a noose tighten around his throat.

♣

Akriti kept her word, about being better, trying harder. In the weeks following their conversation at the hospital, there were no outbursts, no episodes of drama.

However, it had become increasingly clear to Siddhant that they weren't meant to be together. It was true that they weren't destroying each other anymore, that they were amicable – but love wasn't about being able to co-exist amicably with another person. There was no emotional connection or intimacy. She would ask about his day, and talk about his interests, but he could tell that it was just a courtesy. She wasn't ready to take an interest in his interests, she still didn't care – she was simply pretending to.

It wasn't her fault. It was no one's fault that they didn't have feelings for each other. Feelings couldn't be forced. It was, he supposed, possible for two people to have a relationship where everything seemed to fit in theory, work together perfectly, in harmony, and yet for them to have no real connection – a relationship without magic.

That was what it was like with Akriti. Forced, staged. As if they were on a reality show, pretending to be in a happy relationship to fool the viewers. Only, Siddhant and Akriti weren't actually on such a show, and Siddhant couldn't understand why they were doing it.

Sometimes, he would catch Akriti staring at him with a strange look on her face … as if she was wondering the same thing. She hadn't let him go when he'd made it abundantly clear that he wanted out, but she wasn't happy with him either. Siddhant's best guess was that she was with him only because she was afraid of being alone. And pretending to be in love with someone was a much better scenario in her head than being alone.

Priyesh still wouldn't talk to Siddhant. He hadn't been joking about moving out. By the time Siddhant had returned from the hospital, Priyesh and his stuff were already gone. He'd tried to talk to him at the hospital, but the first few times Priyesh had responded extremely formally, as if they were just distant acquaintances. Thereafter, whenever Siddhant approached him, he had been quick to come up with reasons to be somewhere else.

In the end, Siddhant had accepted his fate. He couldn't be friends with Priyesh because he had Akriti in his life, and he couldn't change either of those facts. He felt like he was sleepwalking through his own life, with barely any control over anything anymore.

Sometimes, Siddhant wanted to be with Maahi so badly that his entire being ached with longing. She was the only person he'd ever felt magic with – a real connection, the need to be together, to talk to her, to know about her day, to walk around the city aimlessly with her, to touch her, to make her smile. She was his soulmate. And yet, he couldn't so much as text her.

When Akriti had made it clear to him that she wouldn't let him go, Siddhant had known immediately that he would have to stop talking to Maahi. He couldn't involve Maahi in this madness; she didn't deserve that. And he couldn't give her what she deserved because he didn't have anything to give. His life had been taken away from him.

Six weeks after Siddhant was discharged from the hospital, he found himself sitting in front of the television with Akriti, her head resting casually on his shoulder as if it was the most normal thing in the world.

They were watching an episode of *Black Mirror*, which was one of Akriti's favourite shows. Even though Siddhant's eyes were fixed on the screen, his brain registered none of the moving pictures. He sat there, frozen, unaffected by his surroundings. He couldn't care anymore. His life was a whole other level of nightmare now. He couldn't be with the girl he loved. His best friend had moved out and cut him out of his life. He was being held hostage in this *relationship*, by his 'girlfriend' and he was playing his part of 'boyfriend' because he was terrified that if he didn't obey her wishes, she would harm herself.

Akriti had moved into Priyesh's room. She believed that even though Siddhant and she weren't prepared for physical intimacy, they should be around each other more, and really get a chance to know each other. She had moved in five weeks after she'd tried to kill him with his car, and now Siddhant couldn't so much as sneeze without her knowing.

He was under surveillance, constantly. He felt an iron grip around his throat, lead in the pit of his stomach and his skull was split in two with a headache that never let up. If he left, she would do something very rash, and he would be to blame. He couldn't deal with the weight of that responsibility.

Some mornings, he was too tired to get out of bed. There was no motivation in his life for him to do anything. He didn't want to go to work, he didn't want to talk to anyone, he didn't want to do anything … he didn't want to exist. He had begun to wonder what it would be like to not have to wake up the following morning.

In his attempt to save her life, he had lost his own will to live.

Chapter 18

'What do you want to do tonight?' Akriti called cheerfully from the kitchen. She poured herself apple juice in a tall clear glass.

Siddhant shrugged, too tired for words. He hadn't slept well in weeks. It was Saturday, but he couldn't recall the date. None of those details mattered to him anymore. He didn't have any goals for himself, any interest in anything, any social life, or the desire to even leave the apartment.

'Oh, come on, Sid! Don't be like that!' Akriti complained. 'Let's go see a movie. Is there anything good in theatres right now? Any of those superhero movies you like so much? Thor and Star-God and all that?'

'Star-Lord,' Siddhant corrected automatically. 'And no, no new Avengers movies out right now.'

'Oh good! I didn't really want to have my ears blown up anyway,' Akriti said and laughed, finding herself exceptionally funny. She walked over to him and studied him with her heavily kohl-ed eyes, like he was a child. 'I wish I could find a way to cheer up my baby,' she pouted, tousling his hair. 'Tell me, what do you feel like doing? Anything you want.'

She was behaving as though he was a dog being offered a treat. As though he should feel grateful to be permitted to do what he want with his time for one evening. His captor was keeping him hostage for as long as it took for her to make him fall in love with her. He was being held against his will, blackmailed into it. He was caught in an emotional trap …

Akriti kept speaking, but Siddhant tuned her out. Everything around him faded, and all he could hear was a loud ringing coming from inside his own ears, and all he could see was Maahi's concerned face, asking him if he was being abused, telling him that abuse can be psychological too … asking him if he felt free …

His life had reached a point where he had begun to feel the way Akriti had described feeling the night of the crash. Like he had been forced deep into the ground and had to constantly keep fighting against getting buried in … if he stopped, even for one second, he would drown in mud and never come back up.

The scariest part about it was that sometimes he wondered why he should keep fighting at all. What would happen if he just gave up? What was he fighting *for*? There was nothing he cared about anymore, nothing that made him happy.

And then, he realized something. He missed it … he missed being happy.

Siddhant got up. Barely registering that Akriti was still speaking, he walked into his room and put on a pair of clean jeans. He ran his fingers through his hair before grabbing his keys.

As he crossed the living room, Akriti asked, 'Where are you going?'

'I'm leaving,' Siddhant responded shortly, not slowing down.

'Wait – hold on! What's the rush? Where are you going? When will you be back?' Akriti was following him as he reached the door, an exasperated expression on her face.

'I don't know.' And with that, Siddhant shut the door.

Free.

🌹

After fifteen minutes of driving, his destination became clear to him. He'd wanted to see Maahi, and his body had brought him there. He parked in the same lot where he had bumped into Maahi a few months ago. His steps were determined as he approached her shop and pulled the door open.

And then he was face-to-face with her. She stood there, clutching something that Siddhant didn't pay attention to. She was it. She was his happiness. He needed her, as badly as he needed his next breath of air. She was everything he would ever need. Her brows knitted in confusion when she saw him, her mouth slightly open.

Siddhant's heart raced. What was his plan? What was he going to say? Hey, I'm here looking for happiness? He was suddenly painfully aware of how unprepared he was. From the corner of his eyes, he saw someone move.

'Laila.' He nodded.

'Oh, hey Siddhant. What's up?' Laila said.

'I was in the neighbourhood,' he said a little too quickly.

'Right. Now that you're here, you have to try this rack here – all new recipes, all pretty damn delicious. And we all know how partial you are to Maahi's cupcakes,' Laila said, waving her hand over the glass counter where rows and rows of cookies and cupcakes were on display. 'They're not up for sale yet. Just testing out new stuff.'

'I'll be sure to try some,' Siddhant assured her.

'Hey, Siddhant,' Maahi said, still looking a little confused. 'Just in the neighbourhood, huh?'

Siddhant couldn't look into her eyes and lie to her. Instead he asked, 'How are you?'

'I'm okay. You? I tried calling … but never heard back from you. I went to the hospital too, but they said you were discharged …'

'I'm sorry I didn't tell you. Things have been … complicated. I couldn't talk to you, couldn't involve you in all that.'

'Okay … But, are you okay now? Have you fully recovered?'

'Yes. Yes, I have.'

'Good. That's great,' Maahi said, her relief reflecting in her eyes.

They'd run out of things to say. Siddhant felt the pressure mounting with every second that passed and he didn't speak. Panicking, he said to the room, 'So, do you have plans tonight?'

Maahi pointed to Laila and said, 'We were just going to order in. JD is coming over too. What about you?'

Before Siddhant could respond, Laila said, 'Yeah, you should join us. It's gonna be real fancy. Chinese food.'

'Chinese sounds great, actually,' Siddhant was surprised to hear himself accepting the invitation.

'It's settled then. Also, JD and I have to go to this club opening later. It's really dumb – JD's friend has too much money and dreams of running the best nightclub in south Delhi. I'm expecting there to be plenty of watered-down cocktails and freakishly pink and purple lights that hurt your eyes. Game?'

Siddhant grinned. 'Thanks, but I'll have to pass. That sounds truly awful.'

Laila looked disappointed.

'She's been trying to trick people into coming all day.' Maahi laughed. 'But that was a really bad effort, you didn't even try to sell it,' she said, turning to Laila.

'I'm tired of pretending,' Laila shrugged, disappearing into the back room. She called out to them, 'I just need five more minutes to wrap things up before we leave here.'

'Cool,' Maahi called back. She looked at Siddhant, as if still trying to figure out the reason behind his sudden appearance.

'You do what you've got to do,' Siddhant said coolly, much more composed outside than he felt inside. He took a seat by the window and added, 'I'll wait.'

'Would you like a cupcake while you wait?'

'Yes, please!' he said, suddenly excited. He was transported to two years ago when he had come to see Maahi, under the guise of a love for cupcakes.

Maahi shook her head at him as she walked away. She returned moments later with a selection of cupcakes and set them down in front of him before resuming her work around the bakery. Siddhant bit into a cupcake and was hit with a strong wave of nostalgia. Very few things in the world could compete with Maahi's baking. He ate with more enthusiasm than he had felt for anything in a long long time.

'Wow, when was the last time you ate?' Maahi laughed when she came back a few minutes later and saw that he'd polished off every last crumb.

'I don't know. Last week?' Siddhant muttered, suddenly remembering how depressing his life was without her.

'Are you serious?' Maahi looked confused.

Siddhant shrugged.

'Is everyone ready?' Laila said, digging into her handbag for something.

'Yep,' Maahi said, turning to her. 'Is JD meeting us at the house?'

'I think so. I'm calling him,' Laila said, her phone already glued to her cheek.

'Where is this house you speak of?' Siddhant asked.

'Chanakyapuri. It's Laila's parents' house, actually. But her mom went to Patna to teach at this really good school last year for a few months, and ended up taking a permanent position. This way she can be close to her parents, who are not in the best of health. Laila wasn't happy about her mom abandoning her, but she has me as her roommate instead, so she can't complain,' Maahi said proudly.

Laila rolled her eyes at her, and continued speaking on the phone as the three of them set out together.

❧

The evening ended up being a lot less weird than Siddhant had anticipated. He had driven to Chanakyapuri, following Maahi and Laila's car, cursing himself for committing to this, and freaking out about how awkward it would be. However, once they arrived, and JD joined them, he found himself having a really good time.

He'd met JD once before, at Maahi's birthday party, but hadn't really got a chance to interact with him. JD was a riot – and JD and Laila together were something special. There was never a dull moment. Siddhant had always liked Laila, and was glad to find out that the feeling hadn't changed. She was witty and funny, with a good heart, and he could see how in love JD and Laila were with each other.

After they'd eaten enough, Laila and JD went to get dressed. Maahi and Siddhant just sat back and watched them argue about outfits and traffic and Punjabi music and tequila as they kept disappearing from and reappearing into the room.

Siddhant was nibbling on some fried rice when Laila walked into the living room holding up two dangling earrings. 'These ones?' she said.

'I like them!' Maahi gave her a thumbs-up.

'Mmm, I don't know. They kind of clash with my shoes,' she said to herself and vanished again.

'My hair won't behave. I told you I need a cut,' JD yelled from the other room.

'Don't you dare bring scissors near those beautiful curls,' Laila yelled back.

'Or what?'

'Do you really want to find out?'

There was a pause that suggested JD didn't want to find out. Maahi put a fork-full of noodles in her mouth.

It took Laila and JD a long time to leave the house, but when they did … they were gone. Siddhant abruptly realized that he was alone with Maahi. He'd been too distracted by Laila and JD's shenanigans to think about what he would say to Maahi once they were alone.

Suddenly the air was thick with silence. Maahi looked at him, her mouth slightly open again. He saw the girl he'd fallen in love with two years ago … the girl he'd never stopped loving. Her big, brown eyes, with kindness in them. Her generous spirit. Her good heart. Her fierce ambition. Her unwavering loyalty. It was all there.

She was looking up at him with questions in her eyes. A little confusion, a little sadness.

Siddhant said the words before he could stop himself. 'I love you.'

Her eyes widened in surprise and she inhaled softly. He leaned towards her and pressed a kiss on her lips. Just for a second, just a little touch, and then he pulled back. He looked into her eyes.

'I love you, Maahi,' he said again, and his heart soared.

Chapter 19

'Siddhant,' Maahi whispered.

'I never stopped loving you. I trained myself not to think about you, and tricked myself into believing that I had moved on, but the truth is that I never stopped loving you,' Siddhant confessed. None of his nervousness was evident in his tone. He sounded confident, sure of himself and every word he was saying.

'You're with Akriti.' Maahi let that statement hang in the air. It wasn't a question, she didn't add to it or ask for an explanation. It was a fact.

Siddhant searched for a response to that which wouldn't end the conversation right there. He didn't want to talk about Akriti, not right now. Right now, it was about how he felt about Maahi. 'There are these ... social conventions. These rules and regulations. Binding laws that don't allow us to be ourselves and do what brings us happiness. I refuse to follow them. Not anymore,' he said.

'What are you saying?' Maahi whispered.

'I'm saying that I love you. And nothing else matters to me.'

Maahi was looking at him with an inscrutable expression. He watched as sadness and confusion slowly gave way to realization and … Was that happiness? His heart thumped loudly in his chest, ready to jump out of his body.

'Forget about everything else. The past, the future. Right now, in this moment, how do you feel?' Siddhant asked, his voice shaking. He took her hand, partly in order to stop his own from trembling.

Maahi's face scrunched up, as if she was in agony. 'I'm scared. I don't know what to say …'

'Maahi … do you still care about me?'

'Of course I care about you. What kind of question is that? You *know* that I care about you.'

'Do you still love me?'

There was a pause. She gripped his hand tighter, and her eyes filled with tears. She looked down, causing a teardrop to escape through the corner of an eye, and murmured, 'Yes.'

Siddhant released a deep breath, the air returning to his lungs all at once. His chest rose and fell quickly, as he hooked his finger under her chin and tipped up her face. 'Say it,' he said, his eyes boring into hers, 'please say it.'

'I love you,' Maahi uttered breathlessly.

Siddhant's arms went around her and he pulled her into a crushing hug. Their hearts beat next to each other's, both restless, both soaring. 'I love you … I love you,' he whispered repeatedly with his nose sunk into her hair, breathing her in. It was a wonderful feeling … remembering the feel and the smell from memory, and experiencing it in such vivid detail in the present, all his senses alight.

Maahi's hand, which had been resting on Siddhant's shoulder, slid to his neck, and further up to his jaw. She let it rest there. He could feel his pulse throb under her palm. Her other hand clutched his back. She rested her chin on his shoulder, causing all of her hair to fall forward and cover her face.

Her scent strong in his nose, he inhaled it deeply. The warmth of her body, the steady beating of her heart against his, the way she was holding him … this was his home. *She* was his home. His heart was overflowing with joy. He hadn't felt this exhilarated since … in more than a year.

But in the next second, he felt Maahi stiffen in his embrace. She loosened her grip around him, and pulled back to look at him. Her voice was low. He could barely hear her when she said, 'But what about …? Siddhant …'

'Shh.' Siddhant placed a finger on her lips. 'No buts. Please. Whatever it is – does it matter? In this moment, where there's you and me, and we're here … with each other. Does anything else matter?'

Maahi looked at him for a long moment then slowly shook her head. She relaxed again, and allowed herself to be pulled into another embrace. This time, it was Siddhant who pulled away. He placed both his hands under her jaw, cradling her face. Gazing deeply into her eyes, he leaned closer and touched his lips to hers. Maahi's mouth opened with a soft exhalation. Siddhant locked his lips with hers and kissed her. They didn't come up for air for several minutes. All of Siddhant's senses were awakened. This felt like heaven. His hands slid into her hair and her arms went around him, clasping him to her.

Now that he was kissing her, now that he'd had a taste, he realized he would never have enough. He was breathless, kissing her deeper, terrified that the moment would end, the magic enveloping them would disappear. There was a desperation in the kiss, the kind he'd never felt before.

His hand slid down her back and rested on her waist, urging her closer. Maahi moaned softly and the sound sent a rush of warmth to his extremities. She was clinging to him as desperately as he was to her – the moment was an intoxicating mix of all the sensations they were experiencing in the present and their beautiful memories from their past. He kissed her as though his life depended on it, as if kissing her was the only thing that could save him. He nudged her nose with his, lost in the blissful warmth and softness of her mouth.

'Siddhant …' Maahi murmured.

Siddhant pulled back long enough to ask, 'Yes, Maahi?' before leaning towards her again.

Maahi placed a firm hand on his chest to keep him from kissing her. 'Are we bad people? Is this wrong?'

'This is the only thing that's right. In all the chaos in the world, this is the only thing that makes sense,' Siddhant said passionately, believing every word.

'Oh, Siddhant.' Maahi pulled him back towards her and kissed him urgently.

Siddhant woke up with a smile on his face. It took him a minute to remember where the happiness was coming from. Then his eyes fell on Maahi ... sleeping on her side, her face turned towards him, shining in the morning light. There. She was the source of his happiness.

He watched her for several moments as she slept, her body rising and falling gently with every breath. The curtains on her windows were partially open, casting a glow in the room, lighting up her beautiful face. How could he have let her go? Why hadn't he fought for her when she'd left him?

He cursed himself for his naivety. The night they'd broken up, standing outside her bakery, in the darkness, under the stars, they'd seen no other way. He had felt betrayed by her; she had felt neglected by him. He had been drowning in his medical studies; she'd been struggling to build a sustainable business. The timing was wrong. Breaking up had made sense. It had been easy.

But it had ended up being the hardest thing he'd ever done. He hadn't realized how much he loved her and needed her until she had returned in his life. It was only then that he realized that without her he'd been okay, living, but with her, he felt alive. As if there was a reason, a purpose, something bigger than him at play.

Maahi's eyelids flickered open. She saw him and froze. 'Siddhant.'

'Good morning,' Siddhant said, smiling.

'You have to leave,' she said without preamble. She sat up on the bed, pushed her hair away from her face and tucked it behind her ears. 'Siddhant, you can't be here.'

The magic was over. The bubble had burst. They were back to reality now. Siddhant sat up too and tried to take her hand, but she pulled away. 'Maahi ...'

'You have to go *now*,' she said firmly.

She looked agonized, and Siddhant felt incredibly guilty for causing her to feel that way. He got up from the bed and backed away. 'Okay, I'll go. But can we at least talk before you kick me out?' he said. 'Please?'

'You don't understand. This is not right,' Maahi said desperately, fidgeting with the sleeve of her T-shirt. 'We can't be together. You're in a relationship, for God's sake!'

'It's not a real relationship!'

'Does Akriti know that?' Maahi retorted. 'Whatever it is, it's still a relationship. This is wrong.'

Siddhant changed track. 'I should never have let you go. I know there were problems ... serious problems. But we should've tried to work through them. I should've insisted. It would've been hard ... but being away from you was harder. The hardest thing I've ever had to do ...'

'It doesn't matter anymore!' Maahi said. 'Yes, I've thought about you every single day since we've been apart. Yes, I've missed you terribly. Yes, I've regretted ever letting you go. But none of that matters right now! This is about right and wrong. And us being together like this is *wrong*.'

'Look me in the eye and tell me that it feels wrong to you,' Siddhant challenged.

'It doesn't matter how it *feels*. The fact is that it *is* wrong. It's not just about the two of us. There are other people involved who will get hurt. Akriti will get hurt. If we're going behind her back, keeping her in the dark … How is that not self-serving? I can't do that to her. We can't be deceiving.'

'I don't intend to deceive her. I have every intention of telling her. If you know me at all, you know that I'm not going to lie to her about this. Do you believe me?'

'I do. But I can't be involved in this. Whatever's going on between Akriti and you … I can't help you with it anymore. Not now when … when there's another agenda … I could've helped you as a friend, but we've crossed a line now. It's too complicated. You have to sort it out with her. It's not my place to interfere,' Maahi said, her hand on her forehead, her eyes darting from one object in the room to another, as if trying to collect all of her scattered thoughts.

'I know! I'm not asking you to have a secret affair with me or something. That's not fair to you! You deserve much more. I would never do that to you. Or Akriti,' Siddhant said earnestly. 'I promise you, I will talk to her. I just … I need to figure out how. It's not easy … She's not in a good place.'

Siddhant paused, his heart sinking at the thought of having to go back home to Akriti. What was he going to tell her, and how? What was she going to say?

After a few moments of silence, in which they both battled with their thoughts, Maahi spoke, in a much calmer tone. 'No matter how I see it, I can't reconcile with the fact that by being together, we're causing someone pain. That's not the foundation of a good relationship. It's not the foundation I want to build our relationship on. We've already messed this up once. And this time too it's messy right from the beginning … And that's not okay. Love doesn't look like this. Love should be beautiful. It shouldn't cause someone pain.'

Siddhant nodded, shoving his hands in his pant pockets. He wanted to say something, but words failed him. Nothing he could say would change her mind. He didn't want to change her mind. He didn't want to give her hope when he himself felt so hopeless suddenly. There was nothing to do but leave. When he reached her bedroom door, he turned back to look at her one last time. She was sitting on the bed with her legs folded under her, staring at the floor.

He wanted to ask her to wait for him. But knowing Akriti … what were the chances that this wouldn't hurt her? In the past, she'd lashed out at much smaller things. And this was big, life-changing. His heart sank. Would he ever get his life back? Would he ever be happy again?

Chapter 20

On the drive home, Siddhant tried to think of the best way to tell Akriti. He was worried that she would threaten to harm herself again. He was fairly sure that, having done so once before, she wasn't above blackmailing him again. But it hadn't really worked the last time, had it? She'd made him stay, yes, but couldn't possibly think theirs was a good relationship. Surely, she wasn't happy either.

When he reached home, he still didn't know what he would say; the only thing he had decided on was that he would be firm. He would be kind, and logical, and he would try to make her see reason, but he would stand his ground.

No matter what.

It was a little after 9 a.m. when he unlocked the front door and entered the apartment. He was preparing himself for confrontation but he found confrontation waiting for him. Akriti was sitting at the kitchen counter, her legs crossed, her body turned towards the front door, holding a mug. She was looking straight at him.

'Welcome back,' she said, her lips stretching in a tight smile.

How long had she been sitting there like that, waiting for him like some sort of a sinister villain in a bad drama?

'How was she?' Akriti asked, her eyes narrowed.

'How was who?' Siddhant asked. Who could she possibly be talking about? When he had left home the night before, he himself hadn't known where he was going. How could Akriti?

'The girl you were with. You were with some girl, weren't you?'

'Why would you jump to a conclusion like that?'

'Answer the question.' Akriti gritted her teeth.

'I wasn't with *some girl*. I didn't go out looking to find *some girl*. I was with Maahi,' Siddhant said.

'Maahi?!' Akriti uncrossed her legs and gave Siddhant a steely glare. 'After you explicitly told me there was nothing going on between the two of you? That Maahi?'

'I never lied to you. There wasn't anything going on between Maahi and me—'

'Wasn't? So there is now?'

'No. I mean I don't know. Akriti, I have to talk to you about something,' Siddhant said. He sat down on the chair next to her and spoke calmly. 'We can talk about Maahi if you want, but I need to talk to you about something important first.'

'Well, I want to talk about Maahi!' Akriti's voice was rising.

'Okay, but first listen to me …'

'Are you listening to yourself? You left last evening, without explanation, and didn't come back all night. Like, what the fuck! I was worried sick! What if something had happened to you?'

'I had my phone with me. If you were worried—'

'What? I should've called you? Like some kind of loser chasing after you?' Akriti was screaming now. 'Don't I have any self-respect?'

'I didn't say that. I meant that if you were so worried about me, you could've called me. I never miss your calls, you know that. When have I ever not taken your calls or not responded to your texts?'

Akriti changed track, her voice shaking with anger. 'Why didn't you just tell me where you were going? You could've just told me when you were leaving that you were going to see that whore—'

'Akriti!' Siddhant thundered. 'Do not talk about her like that!'

'Why not? That's what she is—'

Frustrated, Siddhant ran his fingers through his hair. 'Just stop for a second and listen to me, Akriti! Please. Sit back down and hear me out. There is no need to yell or call anyone names. We're both adults, capable of having a reasonable conversation,' he insisted. He couldn't let Akriti's anger distract him. He was determined to make his intentions clear once and for all.

'How can we have a reasonable conversation when you're going to behave like an animal, going behind my back and cheating on me?' Akriti waved her arms madly in the air. 'I can't believe this is happening! How could you do this to me?'

'My intention wasn't to hurt you,' Siddhant said, struggling to keep control. He spoke in a quieter, firmer tone. 'Last night, when I said I was leaving, I meant that I was leaving this ... all of this.' He paused. 'You.'

'You're leaving me?' Akriti was stunned. For a moment, she forgot her anger and studied his face.

'Yes. We can't be together anymore. I've tried to tell you this without hurting you for a long time ... but there isn't any other way. I don't know what else to do but be honest with you. I can't be with you anymore. I really cannot do this,' Siddhant said softly. 'This is the only way either of us can recover from this mess. And I'm not talking about just last night. I'm talking about before that – we've both been unhappy this entire time. We make each other really miserable. And that's no way to live.'

'I make you miserable?' Akriti questioned, the hurt glistening in her eyes.

'I'm not saying it's all you. I'm to blame too. I'm just not strong enough to give you the kind of support you need to recover from your loss. I should've realized that sooner and helped you find someone who could. We've talked about you going to therapy so many times now. Repeatedly. But it hasn't happened. And over time, instead of getting better, things have only become worse ...' Siddhant paused. His thoughts were scattered. He was afraid that words would come out of his mouth in a manner she might find hurtful.

'So you're saying my father dying has been super inconvenient for you, you asshole?'

Siddhant ignored the profanity. 'I'm not saying that at all. I empathize with you and your situation. I care about you and truly feel for you, but no matter how hard I've tried, I've never been able to help you, have I? Maybe in the beginning … I was able to make you feel better momentarily, but that's all. And it wasn't enough.'

'I can be better … I'll go to therapy …'

'You've said that before. But you haven't. And now it's too late. Whatever chance we had to fall in love … we don't anymore. Too much has happened for us to forget and start over now.'

Akriti sat down suddenly as if her legs were no longer able to bear her weight. Siddhant could tell that she was finally listening to him, and capitalized on the moment.

'Akriti, the truth is that we never really loved each other. Ask yourself if you ever truly loved me. Maybe you needed someone, and I was there for you. Maybe some of the feelings we felt were projected. The idea of it was romantic … coming together in this storm. But think back to our first date: Did you feel anything towards me? Did you even like me? Would we have gone on a second date?'

'You never loved me? From day one? You've never even liked me?' Akriti looked at him accusingly.

'I'm saying that things might've played out differently in different circumstances. I don't know. I really have no way of knowing what could've happened. But I can tell you what did happen … Okay, okay, forget about the past and everything else in our lives … Just think about this – why should we stay together now? Why do you want this relationship? Why do you want me in your life?'

'Because you're my boyfriend!'

'Do you just need a boyfriend, or do you need *me*?'

'What kind of a question is that? *You're* my boyfriend. I need *you*,' Akriti cried.

'Okay, then tell me what it is that I have that you want from your boyfriend? Think about it.' When Akriti didn't say anything, Siddhant continued. 'The truth is that you don't even like me. You don't like my friends, you make fun of my interests, you don't want to do the things I like, you have no idea how my relationship with my family is – or anything at all that's important to me. You don't like me or care about me. You don't even know me!'

Siddhant tried not to sound hurt when he said that, but couldn't help it. He'd been suffocating in this relationship for months and months, losing a little bit of himself daily, and never once had she cared enough to take even the slightest interest in his life. Never. Not once had she even asked him how he was doing.

Because she looked so hurt, he continued, 'And I know that it's not necessarily your fault that you've ... that I've been neglected throughout this relationship. I understand your circumstances, I know the state of mind you've been in, and how hard it's been for you ... But whatever the reason is, the truth remains that in all these months that we've been together, you have never cared about me.'

In the stunned silence that followed, Siddhant waited patiently for Akriti to say something, grateful that she was finally paying attention to him. Obviously, he'd given her much less credit than she deserved. For a moment, he relaxed. Maybe things would be okay after all …

And then, the moment passed.

Akriti stood up forcefully, and spat, 'Nice try! First you cheat on me, and then you have the balls to come here and try to turn this around on me? Do you think I'm stupid?'

Siddhant got up too. 'I wanted to talk about why you and I shouldn't be together … the fact that we don't love each other, and are in a dysfunctional relationship. That's what this conversation was about.'

'Right. Because you didn't want to talk about that bitch—'

Siddhant raised his voice enough to drown hers. 'But sure, if you'd rather talk about Maahi, and how I'm in love with her, we can do that too. Just know that these are two separate issues. Even without Maahi in the picture, you and I are still not right for each other. We still make each other miserable. I would still want to break up.'

'Don't try to change the topic! Did you sleep with her?' Akriti cried.

'No. I mean, yes, technically, we fell asleep together, but we didn't *sleep together*,' Siddhant said.

'Oh, please! You expect me to believe that you spent the night with your ex and nothing happened? Do you think I was born yesterday?'

'We kissed.' Even though he was telling the truth, the kisses he had shared with Maahi felt far too special to fall under the mere *we kissed* category.

'Right. And I'm the dumbest girl on the planet,' Akriti snorted. She shook her head angrily. 'Did you think about me at all? Or how I would feel?'

Siddhant paused. He didn't want to hurt her, but he didn't want to lie to her either. He had to be honest. 'No,' he said slowly. 'For once, I only thought about myself. About my own happiness.' He stopped himself from adding *because no one else thinks about it* – that would be too cruel. No one else was responsible for his happiness.

'Wow. Not once! I didn't cross your mind once.' Akriti was crying bitterly, her voice shaking.

'I'm sorry. I'm really sorry. I never meant to hurt you,' Siddhant said sincerely.

That seemed to make Akriti angrier. 'Saying sorry doesn't make things okay! You can't expect to get away with just about anything by saying a stupid sorry. And why the fuck are you so fucking calm?'

She was trying to get a rise out of him, but he stayed firm in his resolve – no matter what happened, he would stand his ground and say everything he had to say. 'Akriti, I care about you, but this had to end. I can't help you by being your boyfriend. We've tried. It doesn't work.'

'You just want to run to *her*.'

'I want to do the right thing. Do you want to be with someone you don't love? Who's in love with someone else? We have to do what's right, for *all of us*.'

'You mean you and her!' Akriti shouted. 'Don't you fucking try to patronize me! Don't pretend to know how

I feel. I love you, and I won't let you go. Do you hear me? You can't leave me; I won't let you!'

Siddhant struggled to maintain his composure. 'You can't keep me against my will. When one person in a relationship doesn't want it anymore, the relationship ends. There is no—'

'No, it doesn't! Not with me. I need you. If you leave me now, and something happens to me … you'll regret it for the rest of your life.' Akriti's voice was eerily calm suddenly. Like it had been the last time she blackmailed him into staying with her by threatening to harm herself.

Siddhant was terrified, but he spoke firmly, 'That is extortion.'

'Are you willing to risk it?' Akriti challenged. 'Imagine tomorrow, you get a call from the hospital …'

'Akriti.' Siddhant couldn't hide his anger. 'If you do something rash, you'll only be proving my point.'

'Oh God! Don't you get it? I don't care. I don't fucking care about anything anymore. What do I have to live for anyway? Everyone I love just leaves me. I have no one. No one! Nobody gives a fuck about me.' Akriti was sobbing.

'That is not true. *I* care about you. You have friends who love and support you. Your stepmom cares about you so much she left no stone unturned to protect you after the crash. You have your career – you're a brilliant doctor. The world needs that,' Siddhant said. He rubbed his forehead and continued gently, 'I want to help you, Akriti, but I can't do that as your boyfriend. As your boyfriend, I somehow always end up being on the opposite team … I don't want that. I want to be on your team.'

'Then why are you leaving me?'

'Because I can't live in fear and misery. I'm drowning. I feel the way you once told me you did, as if I'm being buried alive ...' Siddhant said. A tear escaped the corner of his eye as he looked into her crumpled face. 'I can't keep waiting for something else to happen. Constantly dreading what's coming ... I can't stay with you, constantly dreading ... I'm not equipped to take care of you. You need real help, Akriti. I can help you get it ... but I'm just not the person who can give it.'

'Siddhant ...' Akriti cried, wiping the tear from his face.

He pressed her hand to his cheek for a moment then let it fall to her lap. 'Do you believe me? Please tell me that you believe that I care about you. So much. And you're right. If something happens to you, I'll never recover ... And after I leave, yes, I'll be terrified that you'll do something rash, but the truth is that even if we stay together, there is no guarantee that something bad won't happen ... that I won't be equally terrified ...'

'I'll try to be better ...' Sobs wrecked her body as she spoke, words barely escaping her mouth.

Holding her gaze, he spoke from his heart, 'And I'll help you. I want you to get better, and feel better. I want you to not have to carry this weight of grief you carry around. It's not fair to you. No one should have to experience a loss like that ... but the truth is that all of us do, sooner or later. But there are resources ... people and programmes that can help you. You just have to be brave, and be open to the idea of asking for help—'

Even before he finished speaking, he knew he'd lost her again.

Akriti's jaw tightened, and she stood up. 'I don't need your fucking pity,' she said through gritted teeth and stormed out.

Chapter 21

The following week Siddhant didn't see Akriti even once. He checked her room for signs of activity, but nothing in there had moved since the day they broke up and she had walked out. With every passing hour, he got more and more worried. He tried to ask Prachi, but she didn't give him the time of day. As far as she was concerned, he had wronged her friend and she wanted nothing to do with him. Siddhant was baffled; Prachi was at the party on the night of the crash, she had heard how unreasonable Akriti was being. But she clearly had a different idea of what had happened that night than he did, and he didn't have the energy or the motivation to share his side of the story with her.

He tried to call Maahi, but didn't get a response. So he texted her, to which she simply asked, *Is Akriti okay?* When he said no, she wrote back: *Then I can't do this. I'm sorry.*

Siddhant didn't try to change her mind. She was right. Love was supposed to be beautiful, not hurtful. He didn't want to build a relationship with her on the ruins of another. She deserved better. So, no matter how desperately he wanted to be with her, or how hopeless he felt, he didn't call her.

🌹

When Siddhant entered the cafeteria, he was lost in thought. Two weeks had passed since he had last seen Akriti, and there was still no trace of her. He was miserable, constantly wondering if she was okay, but the fact that there was no news from anyone about her at all provided a little relief – he took it to mean that nothing bad had happened. Because … if it had, they would definitely have heard something …

He picked a chicken sandwich and water and took his tray back to his usual table. Out of the corner of his eye, he spotted Priyesh sitting a few tables away, looking at his phone. On an impulse, Siddhant walked over to him, set his tray on the table and sat down on the seat facing his friend.

'Hi,' Siddhant said, making himself comfortable. He started eating, as if it was the most natural thing to do. 'How's it going?'

'What do you want?' Priyesh said stonily.

'To talk to my friend. And apologize to him.'

'I'm listening.'

'You were right, from the beginning. You were right about Akriti and me being in a loveless relationship, and about her needing help. You were right to suggest that I should break up with her—'

'Don't get me wrong, this is fun, but I didn't hear an apology ...'

'You're such a jerk!'

'Whoa! Literally the worst apology in the history of apologies,' Priyesh said, clearly enjoying himself at Siddhant's expense.

Siddhant took a deep breath. 'I'm sorry. You were right, and I should've listened to you.'

'But instead of doing that, you chose to let that girl do her best to kill us,' Priyesh said seriously. '*And* you let her get away with it! After she did that to us. To you! What was that about not filing an FIR? Did you forget how battered up you were? How our cars never recovered?'

'Akriti's mom did pay for the damage to the cars, and at the end of the day, cars can be replaced. What I'm really sorry for is ... putting you in the line of fire. I could never imagine that you would be caught up in this mess and get hurt. And trust me, it's something I'll always regret,' Siddhant said sincerely.

'Yeah, uh,' Priyesh said, uncomfortable with this show of feeling. 'It's okay. Wasn't your fault. I was just mad that you didn't care about me when you woke up and you know, didn't want revenge or whatever,' he said very fast.

'Valid. From now on, I've got your back,' Siddhant said, trying to sound airy.

'Cool.'

Embarrassed by the honesty and the exchange of emotions, they concentrated on their food for the next few minutes. Siddhant was relieved that Priyesh had forgiven

him, and hadn't asked whether Akriti was still in his life
or not. He didn't know how to answer that question. He
remembered Priyesh's ultimatum full well – that Siddhant
had to choose between him and Akriti.

Siddhant wanted to ask where Priyesh was living, and
whether he would consider coming back, but he couldn't
do that either, since Akriti had moved into Priyesh's room
where all of her stuff still remained. In any case, Siddhant
figured there would be plenty of time to talk about all that.
For now, he was just glad that he could eat lunch with his
best friend.

❧

Three weeks after Akriti disappeared, Siddhant began to
really lose his mind. He couldn't stop thinking about her.
He'd tried reaching out to everyone he could think of –
friends, colleagues, her stepmom – without luck. The people
at the hospital only seemed interested in sensationalizing
the situation for the sake of gossip, never trying to actually
contribute in helping. Her friends had frozen him out,
refusing to talk to him. Her stepmom was unreachable the
few times he tried calling her; nor had she replied to his
fervent messages.

Siddhant didn't know what to do with himself. He went
through his day like a robot, but inside, he was holding on
for dear life. What if something terrible had happened …?

One night after work, unable to control himself, Siddhant
called Maahi. He didn't think about reason or logic. He didn't

consider that nothing had changed since they last spoke, so she was likely to still refuse to speak with him. He simply called her and hoped that she would answer.

'Hi Siddhant,' Maahi said, picking up after four rings.

'Maahi.' He closed his eyes and let the sound of her voice soothe his troubled mind.

'What's going on?'

Her tone was concerned, which he found comforting. However, he wanted to follow her wishes and not involve her in his mess, so he didn't unburden on her.

'I was thinking about you,' he said simply.

'That's sweet,' Maahi said. He could hear her smile through the phone, and it warmed his heart.

'Have you been thinking about me?'

'I've been trying not to ...'

'Is it working?'

'Siddhant,' Maahi sighed. 'You know I can't—'

'I know, I know. Don't say it.'

They stopped talking, but remained on the phone for a few moments. Finally, Maahi asked, 'How is Akriti?'

'I don't know,' Siddhant answered truthfully. 'I haven't heard from her since the night I told her it was over.'

'Did you tell her ... about us?'

'Yes, I did.'

There was a pause. When Maahi spoke finally, Siddhant could hear the fear in her voice. 'Siddhant ... that's not good. Has anyone else heard from her? Oh God ...'

'Listen, Maahi. Don't worry about her. I shouldn't have said anything,' Siddhant said. 'There's no reason to be concerned. I'm sure she just needed some time away from me to think. I'm sure she's okay.'

Siddhant spoke with way more conviction than he felt, cursing himself for telling Maahi anything. It wasn't her problem and she shouldn't have to feel responsible. If there was anyone to blame, it was he. He was the one who'd gone to see Maahi while he was still in a relationship.

'Are you sure?' Maahi asked, sounding uncertain.

'Please don't worry. I shouldn't have called you. I'm sorry for involving you in this mess. I just … needed to hear your voice,' he confessed.

'Siddhant …' Maahi sounded pained.

Siddhant gulped and hung up. He felt completely helpless. His life was crumbling around him. He would be responsible for what happened to Akriti. He couldn't be with the love of his life. He couldn't even breathe.

❦

Another week passed, bringing no news of Akriti. Siddhant was doing worse than ever. He was barely getting any sleep, he was sleepwalking through his job, giving up important cases because he lacked confidence in himself and had no appetite. It had come to a point where even his parents – the last people he would expect to have a clue about his emotional state – had noticed that something was off.

Some mornings, he could barely make it out of bed. He was crippled by constant terror. It had been a month since she'd been gone …

How could no one know anything? Why was no one else worried? She had been away from the hospital without any information for a month, in which time she hadn't reached out to anyone at all. His cause for alarm was valid.

Siddhant had thought about going to the police several times. Should he speak to Akriti's stepmom before going to the police station? Since she was Akriti's only relative, she must be the one to ...

Siddhant paused.

When Akriti's stepmom had come to Delhi after the car crash, she had gone above and beyond to protect Akriti. She'd covered the damages to their cars, begged and pleaded with Priyesh not to file the FIR, posted Akriti's bail and been by her bedside the entire time. She herself had admitted to him that she cared about Akriti deeply and wouldn't let anything harm her.

If Akriti really was missing for a month, how could she not be panicking? How had she not called the police herself?

She knows where Akriti is!

Siddhant picked up his phone and called her. This time when she didn't take his call, he called again. And again. And again. He refused to be kept in the dark any longer. After several calls, he texted her.

Is she okay?

He waited with bated breath for her response, which didn't come. He resumed calling her repeatedly, throughout the day. In the end, he concluded that she must not have her phone with her. How crazy would he look when she returned home at the end of the day, and found thirty-seven missed calls from her stepdaughter's ex?

Feeling stupid, he texted her one last time before leaving for the police station.

Sorry about the calls. I'm really worried about Akriti.
I don't think she's okay, so I'm going to the police now.

Fifteen minutes later, on his way to the police station, when he checked his phone at a red light, he had a text message from Akriti's stepmom.

She's making progress.

Chapter 22

Siddhant felt a rush of relief course through his veins. *She's making progress.* She was with her stepmom, and she was doing better. His hands were shaking too much for him to keep driving, so he pulled over to the side of the road and rested his head on the steering wheel.

She's making progress.

It took him several minutes to calm down and absorb that nugget of information, and realize how it affected various aspects of his life. He could let his anxiety go. He could breathe freely again, sleep again, think again. And once he could think again, the first person he thought of was Maahi.

Without consciously deciding to do so, he found himself driving to her house. He was beaming when he rang the doorbell, but it was Laila who opened the door.

'What's got you down?' Laila raised an eyebrow sarcastically.

'Hi Laila! How great is this evening?'

'Clearly greater for you than for me. Come in,' Laila said, walking back into the living room where there were piles of documents spread out on the floor. 'We're currently buried under this heap of paperwork from Roast House, which we have to get through by tonight.'

Siddhant wasn't listening. Maahi was sitting on the floor with her legs crossed, her long hair a mess, a focussed expression on her face as she studied the paperwork. When she looked up and saw him there, her face changed. She got up quickly and asked in a panicked voice, 'What is it? What happened? Is Akriti okay?'

Siddhant had barely opened his mouth when she spoke again.

'Has she come back? Do you know where she is?' she asked frantically.

'No, I—'

'Then I have nothing to say to you. You have to leave,' Maahi said firmly.

'But listen to me—'

'No. It was wrong of me to get involved with you when I knew you had a girlfriend. And now she's been missing ever since you told her about us. No, no, no. You have to go. Go before we make the situation any worse.'

'Maahi, I couldn't reach her, but—' Siddhant tried to tell her about the text message he got from Akriti's stepmom, but Maahi talked over him.

'Fine, if you won't leave, I will.' With that, she disappeared into her bedroom.

Once she was gone, Siddhant looked at Laila, who had been watching their exchange quietly. She seemed hesitant at first, but then said, 'I agree with her. She doesn't want to be the other woman. Who would? She deserves better.' As an afterthought she added, 'No offense.'

'None taken. I agree. She's not the other woman. She's the only woman,' Siddhant said. 'I heard from Akriti's stepmom. Akriti's making progress.'

'Oh, that's wonderful! Should've led with that.'

'She wouldn't let me speak!'

'Yeah, well. She's been struggling with this a lot. Seeing you again after the break-up brought up emotions and regrets and all that. Then she realized that you'd moved on with someone else. Then you were in that car crash. Then she became the other woman and the main woman, upon finding out about this, went missing. Phew! I'd be freaking out too,' Laila said.

'She felt emotions and regret when she saw me again? When she saw me with Akriti that day at the parking lot?' Siddhant asked.

'You didn't know that?' Laila looked puzzled. She said, mostly to herself, 'Wait, was I not supposed to say that?'

Siddhant experienced another rush of emotion. He felt light-headed with happiness, and muttered, 'I need to talk to her.'

'Good idea. I need to shut up anyway,' Laila said.

Siddhant knocked on Maahi's door before pushing it open. She looked up at him from her bed, and it brought back memories of the last time he was there, when she'd kicked him out. Before she could say anything, Siddhant said, 'Akriti's making progress.'

Maahi's open mouth, clearly planning to say something else, paused. She blinked and asked, 'What? What does that even mean?'

'That's all I know – that she's making progress. Her stepmom texted me. See.' Siddhant walked up to her and showed her the message on his phone.

Maahi's body went limp with relief. 'Oh thank God,' she said, hiding her face in her hands, breathing deeply. 'Thank God she's okay.'

'This is probably not the most romantic way to say this,' Siddhant said, sitting down next to her on the bed, 'but I love you, and I was hoping you would take me back. Please and thank you.'

'Huh?' Maahi looked up from her hands.

'I'm serious. I'm in love with you. Always have been. And I don't want to waste anymore time not being with you.

'For months I was unable to take charge of my life, make my own decisions – decisions for my own happiness. I was failing terribly, with Akriti, in providing what she needed. And I was so focussed on making sure she was okay, that I forgot about myself and what *I* want. It's been clear to me for a long time now that I want to be with you. I love you, Maahi. And now I finally have the freedom …

'And it was you who helped me see that I wasn't free. You came to the hospital and asked me the hard questions that I needed to ask myself. You were right – I wasn't free. It was easy for someone like Priyesh, on the outside, to say that I should leave her and move on but when you're involved in it … you can't. I genuinely care about her, and didn't want to cause her anymore pain than she'd already endured. I couldn't just leave her. There's a good human under all of that … that craziness. And it wasn't her fault, it wasn't her intention to hurt us. I understood that. And I wanted to help that human, and to do so, I had to overlook the behaviour, set it aside as a mere symptom.'

'You're a good person.' Maahi was watching him with pride in her eyes. 'But I wanted you to see that you can be of no help to others, if you don't take care of your own self first.'

Siddhant took her hands and brought them to his lips. He kissed them and said, 'Thank you.'

'Shut up! Don't thank me!' Maahi said. Her eyes were shining with tears when she rested her forehead against his and whispered, 'You have no idea how horrible it was for me to see you in that hospital bed. I was so scared I'd lose you ... even though I'd already lost you ...'

'You never lost me,' Siddhant said firmly. 'I should never have let you go in the first place. It was the dumbest thing I've ever done.'

Maahi was shaking her head against his. 'No, we needed the distance. We broke up for a reason. We had issues that we needed to resolve before we could be with each other. Now that I'm saying it, I wonder if we should've made one of those cheesy pacts they make in movies – where they decide to take a break, do their own thing, but fix a time and a place to meet each other in the future and see how things go.'

'Knowing that we would get a second chance in the future definitely would've helped. It was so hard to be without you. And you know what's funny? When we broke up, we were so certain that it was the only thing to do. I needed to devote time to my studies and work, you needed to devote time to your new business and get over ...' It pained Siddhant to even think of Kishan's name. He tried to sound nonchalant when he said, 'What's the update there, by the way?'

Maahi smiled, but said sincerely. 'Didn't think about him once. He occupies zero per cent of my headspace.'

'Right. Zero is good.' Siddhant tried to hide his relief before continuing, 'Anyway, so as I was saying ... we thought we *had* to break up. But the more I think about it, the more I've realized that that's a bag of trash. The timing will never be perfect!'

Maahi nodded slowly. 'You're right. When we bumped into each other again, the circumstances were the opposite of perfect. Certainly not the *right* time.'

Siddhant pulled away and looked at her beautiful, distressed face, 'Maybe this time, we don't let timing or circumstances determine our destiny. I know the circumstances aren't ideal right now, but they might never be! And that's not reason enough to keep us apart.'

Maahi was quiet, as if mulling over what he was saying.

'I never stopped loving you,' she said finally. 'I fooled myself into thinking I'd moved on, drowned myself in work, but I always thought about you. In the year that we were apart, I thought about reaching out to you so many times. But I stopped myself every time ... because I had done you wrong. It was my fault we broke up, and I was pretty sure you hated me.' Maahi's voice got smaller towards the end.

'Hated you? I could never hate you!'

'But I ... I ruined everything. Yes, we had other problems. We were both in a major time crunch, we were both stressed out – and because of that, we let our relationship become ...

ordinary. It wasn't special anymore. We took each other for granted, stopped putting any effort into us. But I put the final nail in the coffin … when I let Kishan kiss me. I broke your trust. I was disloyal,' Maahi said, her expression pained. She looked away from Siddhant. In a soft, low voice, she asked, 'Will we ever be able to get past that? Right now, we're feeling all these emotions, we're excited about having each other back, but what happens once the honeymoon phase ends? What happened, what I did, it'll always remain … Will you ever be able to forgive me?'

Siddhant sat back, resting against the headboard of her bed, as he collected his thoughts. He spoke slowly, choosing his words carefully. 'I've had a lot of time to think about this, Maahi. Relationships are messy. Love is messy. Just because our brains decide that two people have separated, doesn't mean the people involved will immediately stop having feelings for each other. When you talk about being disloyal … I never thought of you like that. I've always thought the exact opposite, actually, that you're fiercely loyal. You protect the people you care about, you go out of your way to help them … you have very strong loyalties.'

He paused. It still wasn't easy for him to think or talk about Kishan. Eventually, he said, 'When you broke up with Kishan, you tried so hard to move on and immerse yourself into the new life you'd built that you never really *got over* what happened with him. There was no closure, as they say. So when he came back, there were mixed feelings, confusion,' Siddhant shook his head. 'Whatever you want to call it. I don't know. All I know is that if you were disloyal, you would've tried to hide it from me. Instead you told me immediately. And that's a sign of trustworthiness.'

Maahi sighed deeply. 'I was so upset with myself for letting you come over the other night. I didn't want you to betray Akriti's trust. I've been there, and it is the worst feeling in the world. I didn't want you to feel like that.'

'With Akriti … it was different. I know relationships have rules, but kissing you that night … it didn't feel wrong. Not for one second. It felt like the only thing that was right.'

'But it hurt her to find out about it …' Maahi was clearly still struggling with this.

Siddhant didn't want to say anything bad about Akriti, so he tried to explain it in a respectful manner. 'Yes, it did hurt her. But it wasn't because I kissed you. It didn't have anything to do with you, or even me. It was because I left, and I told her that it was over … she would've been angry regardless. Because I left even after she'd played every card to ensure that I would stay. It was about her ego, her pride, her stubbornness.' Siddhant sighed. 'If you zoom out of the situation a little, you will see that in the long run … if you and I are meant to be together – if she was just a chapter and you are the book – then kissing you that night was the right thing to do. I don't regret it.'

Maahi looked into his eyes, a slow smile spreading across her face as she said, 'I don't regret it either.'

'Good,' Siddhant said, planting a kiss on her nose. 'So, let's do it again?'

The sound of Maahi's laughter was heaven to his ears, before he drowned it in his kisses.

Chapter 23

If Siddhant had expected that knowing Akriti was making progress would help him forget about her and move on, he was wrong. The three words Akriti's stepmom texted him weren't enough to keep him from worrying about her. He still woke up in cold sweat, he still found himself wondering what *making progress* meant.

A month after the text message from her stepmom, Akriti still hadn't come back to work. Medical residents in no part of the world could take that kind of time off. At least not without life-or-death reasons. Was Akriti's situation life or death?

The question haunted him. He tried frequently to reach out to her, but so far, his attempts were met with dead silence. Ensuring Akriti's well-being was important to both Siddhant and Maahi – not only because they felt responsible for her pain in some way but also because they believed that she was a good person, caught in a bad situation.

Then, one day, Siddhant came home to find Akriti sitting at the kitchen counter, just like the last time he had seen her. She was wearing blue jeans with a white T-shirt. Her hair was pulled back and she wasn't wearing any make-up.

A long-stemmed white rose lay on the counter. The most striking thing about her appearance was her smile, which he'd only seen on very rare occasions. This time, finding her sitting there by herself, waiting for him to walk in through the door didn't, somehow, feel creepy at all.

'Akriti,' he breathed, surprised. She looked good – happy, healthy.

'Hi, Sid,' Akriti said. She got up and held out the white rose to him. 'Peace offering,' she explained.

Siddhant took the rose from her, still in shock. 'How are you? How have you been?' he asked. 'I tried to call you.'

Akriti laughed, a light, playful chuckle. 'I know. A *couple* of times.'

Siddhant felt embarrassed. He must've called a hundred times, if not more, in the two months since she'd left.

'Careful, Sid, if I didn't know better, I might think you liked me or something,' Akriti said. Her smile dimmed slightly when she added. 'But I appreciate the persistence. You didn't give up. I thought you'd be so glad to be rid of me, you'd never look back. But you surprised me. You really did care, huh?'

'Yes. I still do. And I'm sorry for the way things ended. I never meant to hurt you in any way.'

Akriti held up her hand. 'No need. If someone needs to apologize, we both know it's me.' She motioned to the couch. 'Should we sit? I want to catch up.'

Siddhant sat down, setting the rose on the centre table.

'There are two things I need to do,' Akriti began. 'First, I need to apologize to you, for what I put you through.

Some of the things you said that day ... I was so stupid not to have seen what I was doing to you. Once I calmed down, and thought about it, I realized that you were right about some things. I ... I'm not proud of trying to emotionally blackmail you into staying with me. I was just so terrified of being alone ... When you said it was over between us, all I could see was darkness, and I panicked. I'm so sorry.'

Siddhant nodded. 'It's okay. I understand what you were going through, how you must've felt.'

'Look at you, still sparing my feelings.' Akriti smiled gratefully. 'Which brings me to the second thing – I need to thank you for everything you did for me, despite everything I did to you. You never stopped seeing the best of me, and giving me the benefit of the doubt, no matter how much I pushed you and wrecked your life.

'Oh God, the car crash ... I can never apologize enough for that. I thank God every single day that you made it to the other side okay, and that Priyesh wasn't hurt ... When I think about how much worse it could've been ...'

Her voice caught, and she cleared her throat before continuing, 'Most guys would've just said *this girl is crazy* and moved on, but you kept trying. I gave you more than enough reasons to walk out, but you stood by me. And I needed that more than I realized. I needed someone to show me that I mattered, that I was cared for, that I wasn't absolutely alone in the world. And you did. You were always there, even when I was such an asshole to you.' Akriti was crying, her eyes unfocussed, as if remembering the incidents she was referring to.

'Hey, don't worry about it,' Siddhant said softly. 'It's in the past. And I always knew that even though your anger was directed towards me, it wasn't *about* me.'

'Good, because I need you to know that, okay? It was never about you. You were wonderful, and you didn't deserve that treatment,' Akriti said firmly.

'Thank you for saying that.'

'Thank you for helping me. I don't know where I would've been without that ...'

'So, where exactly were you?' Siddhant asked. 'If you don't mind me asking.'

'Amritsar, with my mom!' Akriti said, her face shining through the tears.

Siddhant noticed that she called her stepmother *mom*.

'What you said to me that day ... about my mom going above and beyond to protect me after the crash ... I didn't know about any of that. I didn't know that she'd convinced you and Priyesh to not file the FIR against me, or paid for the damage I caused to both the cars. And that made me think about all the things she'd done for me over the years, that I've ignored,' Akriti said sadly. 'And I guess I didn't care before, when my dad ... was alive, but with him gone ... I never stopped to think about how lonely my mom must be. They didn't have any kids, you know? I'm all she has, and when you told me everything she did for me, I knew where I had to go. Not that there was anywhere else for me to go. There's something about going home when you're wounded ...'

Siddhant felt a pang of guilt. 'I'm sorry that I hurt you. I know some of the things I said were really harsh, and I shouldn't have said them like that ...'

'No, stop. I'm not going to pretend that your sleepover with your ex didn't hurt me,' Akriti said, sounding bitter for the first time. 'Because that would be a lie. But who am I to stand in the way of true love ... or whatever.'

'Akriti ...'

'I don't want to talk about it. You would've broken up with me regardless, as you should've, so it's a moot point. I don't care,' she said dryly. Despite her insistence, it sounded like she did care, and that he had truly hurt her.

'I'm really sorry.'

Akriti shrugged. 'It's fine. It's good actually – this way, at least some of the blame for our relationship going up in flames goes to you. Balances out the scales a little.'

'If that's how you want to look at it,' Siddhant said.

'Anyway, so I went back to my mom, and we ... resolved some things that were long overdue. And, you'll be happy to know, I'm going to therapy now—'

'That's great!' Siddhant said, cutting her off.

'Wow. I might take the excitement personally.' Akriti laughed, but went on, 'You were right. I needed help. So, I went to therapy, and it's been good. I've only had a few sessions ... but I guess what's helped me more is being with my mom, and letting go of all the resentment and negative feelings I had towards her. We talk about dad often ... I always thought I knew him so well, but there are so many things I didn't know about him. I'm glad that I get to talk about him with someone who knew him well too. I think that's what's helped me the most, you know?'

Siddhant nodded.

'Anyway,' she said abruptly, 'I think that's all. My therapist gave me this homework – I'm supposed to tie up loose ends, apologize, thank people – all that stuff. So, Sid, I'm sorry, and I'm thankful – both beyond measure.'

'Wow, you said that without rolling your eyes.'

'Be serious,' she chided. 'I'm here for selfish reasons – I need to know that you forgive me, so that I can get closure and move on. Okay? Let's try again. I'm sorry and I thank you.'

'It's okay, and I appreciate it,' Siddhant said.

'Great! I'll send movers to pick up my stuff and clear out that room,' Akriti said and got up. 'Must go. Hate goodbyes. Just give me half a hug and get it over with.'

Siddhant smiled, and got up too. But there were no half measures in the hug he gave her. He could feel her body begin to tremble as he held her, and her arms tighten. When she released him, he heard her sniff quietly before she turned away from him, muttering, 'Goodbye, Sid.'

'Bye, Akriti,' he said to her retreating back.

And just like that, she was gone. He picked up the peace offering she'd left behind. The last white rose.

Epilogue

Three months after moving out from Sid's apartment, Akriti returned to her job at the hospital. It had been a crazy year, full of very low lows and very few highs. She'd lost a parent, which had left a permanent ache in her heart, but in the past four months, she had found a parent too.

Thinking about her mom brought a smile to her face. Their relationship had changed so drastically, so wonderfully. They'd developed a deep bond, strengthened by their love for the man they'd both lost. As much as her heart ached when they talked about him, it was also cathartic, and over time, thinking about him had become easier. Of late, she'd been able to remember him without feeling sadness.

The long sabbatical she'd taken from work had helped her recalibrate. She didn't love therapy, but, over time, she had come to hate it less. It was painful to bring up emotions she was trying so desperately to push down, week after week. But she couldn't deny that it was helping her centre herself. She felt well adjusted, or at least *better* adjusted, ready to face the world again.

But she also felt anxious about returning to work. The hospital hadn't been pleased with her break, but they'd eventually been convinced that her reasons were valid. However, work wasn't the only reason why she was nervous about returning to the hospital. She couldn't care less about the fact that her co-workers must've been talking about her behind her back. What gave her anxiety was facing Sid again …

After all they'd been through, she was surprised by how civil their last interaction had been. Breaking up was the right decision for them, their relationship didn't work – she knew all of this, but emotions don't understand reason. She'd wanted to shut her ears to the sound of him talking about Maahi. She still couldn't picture Sid and Maahi together without feeling hurt and angry, but she had found a way to live with it.

However, it was going to be hard to do that now that she had returned to Delhi. It was going to be even harder to be around him again, because regardless of what he thought, for a moment there, she had really loved him. But no matter how hard it was going to be, she knew she was up to it. And if she were to find out that she wasn't … she would learn to be okay.

Just as she was about to make her way to the locker room, she noticed Sid, standing across the corridor with Priyesh and two other people, all looking down at something on the iPad Sid was holding. Her heart twisted. She would never forget what she had done to Sid and Priyesh; she would always regret it.

Sid looked up. Akriti caught her breath when his eyes met hers. He looked surprised for a moment, and then he smiled and waved at her.

Small steps, deep breath, she told herself. She would be okay. It wouldn't happen in a day, or in a week, but it would happen. She would be okay.

Akriti waved back, before turning away and heading towards the lockers. She had a surgery to get to.

Author's note

From the moment it was conceived, the central theme of *The Reason Is You* was simple – it would be a book about being with someone who's dealing with depression. The challenge of loving someone, taking care of them, shouldering the responsibility of their happiness, and how it can change a person when they constantly have to put their own well-being and happiness on the back burner, how overwhelming it can become to try to help someone they're not equipped to help.

As a society, we don't take depression (and mental health, in general) as seriously as we should. We don't pay attention to it. Worse, we diminish it. We think a depressed person can simply *choose* to not be depressed anymore – snap out of it, smile, stop making others uncomfortable with their sadness.

Another concept central to *The Reason Is You* is the conventions of a relationship between two people – how we're supposed to behave in a relationship, what our roles and responsibilities are, what are the boundaries that society has set? I wanted to write about how our ideas of right and wrong tend to take precedence over our true desires in our relationships, but how, if we're brave, we can make decisions that are right for us as individuals, even if they don't feel like the *right* thing. What Siddhant says to Maahi in the end summarizes this accurately: *If you and I are meant to be together – if she was just a chapter and you are the book – then kissing you that night was the right thing to do.*

When I finished writing *Like a Love Song*, which ended with Maahi and Siddhant breaking up, I knew I had to revisit their relationship, put them in a new setting, add fresh perspectives to both of them, give them a second chance and see where it went. There was too much love between them for the story to be over.

While *Like a Love Song* is from Maahi's point of view, in *The Reason Is You* I was intrigued with the idea of writing from a man's perspective – taking a closer look into Siddhant's mind.

As nervous as I was about tackling a sensitive topic like depression, and writing from a male perspective, the thrill and challenge of inspecting the boundaries of relationships and giving Maahi and Siddhant a second chance balanced out the scales. (Who am I kidding, I cried frequently during the process of writing this book; it was hardly a cakewalk.)

One of the hardest parts of this book was writing the character of Akriti. I wanted to be good to her, but not at the cost of authenticity. I wanted her experience, her emotional upheaval, her mood swings, to feel real. I wanted the book to be messy, uneven – to reflect Akriti's state of mind.

I also wanted readers to think about various possibilities, how one detail can affect the rest of the equation, how things would be if the opposite had happened. Was Siddhant the reason Akriti could initially cope with the loss of her father? Or did his support handicap her and stop her from seeking professional help sooner? Was Akriti the reason Siddhant couldn't be with Maahi when he wanted to? Or was her poor treatment of him what prompted him to seek out Maahi and fall in love with her again? Did Siddhant's new relationship with Maahi add to Akriti's grief? Or did it lessen Akriti's guilt a little, knowing that Siddhant was finally happy now, even though it was with someone else?

The grass is always greener on the other side, but we're on *this* side, so we should try to water the grass on our side. Yet, when things don't go our way, we start to look for reasons for our happiness/unhappiness, for someone or something to blame. Which brings me to my last point – our inclination to find reasons to be happy *outside* of ourselves. Should we be searching for reasons to be happy in someone else, or should we be turning inwards? Because maybe, the reason is you.

Acknowledgements

I wasn't in a good place, emotionally, when I wrote this book. Physically, I was at home, living with my family, after having lived alone for a year in New Delhi and then four years in New York. But it was being at home physically that helped me get better emotionally, gain perspective and revaluate things.

So first and foremost, I want to thank my family. Maa, Papa and Bhaiya – you are the best mother, father and brother a girl could ask for. You have the biggest hearts and the most selfless, generous and unconditional way of loving and caring – and I'm not just saying that. I've met a lot of people; the world is not a kind place. Also, Maa, I forgive you for the weight I gained while I was home.

The people who are my home away from home: Sandra Meijer-Polak, the Betty to my Veronica, but with reversed personalities; Yannick Meijer, whose company I've learned to endure; Nejla Ašimović, the constant words of support and annoying positivity in my ears; Nick Sheridan, for always telling me I can do it, even on days when I felt like I literally can't even; Ritu Sirkanungo, for watching the cheesiest movies with me; Laura Marston, traditionally my first reader, who I forgot to send the manuscript to this time.

My team: my agent Anish Chandy, who I couldn't do this without; Swati Daftuar, who did an extraordinary job editing this book; Shatarupa Ghoshal, who cleaned up my mess, AKA copyedited my manuscript; Shabnam Srivastava, who I'm excited to tour the country with again; Ananth Padmanabhan, who takes me out for the best Asian food; Isha Nagar, who designed this gorgeous book cover.

My readers: those who are picking up my book for the first time, and especially those who keep reading my books and write to me with the most generous compliments and the most interesting observations.